ZHANG JIE was born in 1937. At school she was deeply interested in literature, but was persuaded to study economics as being of more use to her country. Upon graduating from the People's University (Beijing), she worked for some time in an industrial bureau, then in a film studio. She did not start to write until after the fall of the Gang of Four in 1976. She is now a full-time writer and one of China's most popular authors.

The first story she ever wrote, 'The Child From the Forest', won a prize in 1978 as one of the best short stories of that year. Since then she has written many stories, essays and novellas. A recent work, 'The Time Is Not Yet Ripe', won the National Best Story Award for 1984 and *Leaden Wings* won China's prestigious Mao Dun Literary Prize in 1985. Zhang Jie is a member of the Chinese Writers' Association and now works for the Beijing branch of the China Federation of Literary and Art Circles.

A firm believer in socialism, Zhang Jie joined the Chinese Communist Party at an early age. During the Cultural Revolution, however, she was fiercely criticized, and much of her writing today is still considered extremely controversial. Through such works as 'Love Must Not Be Forgotten' (1979) and 'The Arc' (1981) Zhang Jie has highlighted the discrimination against women in Chinese society and all her work reflects her preoccupation with social problems and social change.

GLADYS YANG was born in Beijing of missionary parents. She was educated in England and was the first undergraduate to read Chinese at Oxford. She met her future husband, Yang Xianyi, at Oxford and married him in China in 1940. Since 1950 she has worked as a translator at Beijing's Foreign Languages Press and in her distinguished career has translated many important works of Chinese literature. She was imprisoned for several years during the Cultural Revolution, but is now an honoured figure on the Chinese literary scene and, with her husband, makes an invaluable contribution to the fostering of Sino-British cultural relations. They live in Beijing with one of their granddaughters.

Leaden Wings

ZHANG JIE

Translated and with a Preface by
Gladys Yang

Afterword by
Delia Davin

Dedicated to those working selflessly to
invigorate the Chinese nation

Published by VIRAGO PRESS Limited 1987
41 William IV Street, London WC2N 4DB

First published in China 1980 by the People's Literature
Publishing House, Beijing
Copyright © Zhang Jie 1980

Translation and Introduction copyright © Gladys Yang 1987
Afterword copyright © Delia Davin 1987

British Library Cataloguing in Publication Data

Zhang, Jie
    Leaden wings.
    I. Title
    895.1'35[F]   PL2929.5.H2

    ISBN 0–86068–759–7
    ISBN 0–86068–764–3 Pbk

Typeset by Goodfellow and Egan, Cambridge
Printed in Great Britain by
Anchor Brendon, Tiptree, Essex.

List of principal characters in order of appearance

Autumn – Ye Zhiqiu, a journalist.

Mo Zheng, Autumn's adopted son.

Jade – Liu Yuying, a hairdresser who lives in the same block.

Old Wu – Wu Guodong, Jade's husband, a worker at the Dawn Works.

Bamboo – Xia Zhuyun, Zheng's wife, a minor official but rarely goes to work.

Zheng Ziyun – Old Zheng, a vice-minister in the Ministry of Heavy Industry.

Yuanyuan, daughter of Zheng and Bamboo.

Ho Jiabin, an honest outspoken official in the ministry.

Feng Xiaoxian, director of political work in the ministry, a conservative.

Grace – Li Ting, a malicious section chief whose husband is an invalid.

Shi Quanqing, an unctuous official in the ministry who is trying to join the Party.

Guo Hongcai, an enemy of Grace's in the Party branch.

Luo, Grace's ally in the Party branch.

Commissioner Fang – Fang Wenxuan, senior to Feng in the ministry and better-educated. Loves Joy but won't leave his wife.

Joy – Wan Qun, a widow who works in the ministry.

Wang Fangliang, another vice-minister, a modernizer, cynical but cheery.

Tian Shoucheng, the Minister, an old fashioned political type who finds the new policies threatening.

Chen Yongming, manager of the Dawn Works.

Radiance – Yu Liwen, a doctor, married to Chen.

Li Ruilin, a former workshop Party secretary, demoted by Chen.

Old Lü, a janitor at the Dawn Works.

Lü Zhimin, a worker, son of Old Lü.

Yang Xiaodong, a team leader at the Dawn Works.

Miao Zhuoling, the new head of number 4 workshop.

Ge Xinfa
Wu Bin   } workers in Yang's team.
Young Song

Lin Shaotun, secretary to Minister Tian.

Xiao Yi, second secretary to Minister Tian.

Ji Hengquan, secretary to Vice-minister Zheng.

Commissioner Song – Song Ke, the ex-manager of the Dawn Works, bears a grudge against Zheng.

Kong Xiang, an extremely conservative vice-minister, junior to Zheng whom he opposes.

Foreword

What is life?
A friend tells me, 'Life means finding happiness in hardships.' 'No!' I say. 'Life is an endless battle with fate.'

Translator's Preface

Zhang Jie is one of China's most interesting and controversial writers. She was born in 1937 in Beijing. Her father, a minor civil servant, and her mother, a teacher, separated when she was a child. She read voraciously at school and wanted to specialize in literature, but like many idealistic youngsters of her generation was induced to study a subject 'of more use' to the building of socialism, and graduated in 1960 from the Economics Department of the People's University. For some years she worked in the National Bureau of Mechanical Equipment, where she gained considerable knowledge about industry as well as human nature. But literature continued to be her main interest.

She did not begin to write till she was forty, just after the fall of Jiang Qing's Gang of Four. In 1978 she joined the Writers' Association; in 1980 she joined the Chinese Communist Party; and in 1982 she became a salaried member of the Beijing Branch of the China Federation of Literary and Art Circles, able to devote all her time to writing.

Between 1949 and 1977 there had been pressure on Chinese writers to gear their writing to the current ultra-Left political line, and subjects such as democracy, love unrelated to revolution, or the value of the individual were virtually taboo. The Third Plenary Session of the Party in 1978 condemned the previous ultra-Left line and called for a realistic approach to China's problems. It was said that practice was the criterion of truth, which should be sought from the facts. This encouraged writers to write more honestly and tackle a wider range of themes. It was under these circumstances that Zhang Jie began to write, addressing herself to a number of social problems.

The story that brought her into the public eye was 'Love Must Not Be Forgotten'. The Chinese media often imply that an individual's highest fulfilment comes from serving the people and making a contribution to the country. In 'Love Must Not Be Forgotten' Zhang Jie argues that this is not enough. The quality of life depends to a great extent on personal relations, and marriage is crucially important. In China all men and women are expected to marry. But what if you cannot find a congenial partner? The narrator of Zhang Jie's story is in this dilemma. At thirty she is practically 'on the shelf', yet has no potential husband she can love and respect. She finally decides to remain single if no kindred spirit appears despite social disapproval. Chinese moral values today are a mixture of socialist ethics and traditional conventions. And nowhere is the influence of tradition stronger than in the field of marriage. The mother of the narrator was a divorcee who till the end of her life was passionately though platonically in love with a married man, who returned her love at a distance. Her daughter therefore questions the current marriage conventions which inhibit genuine personal affection, and hopes that they will have changed by the time socialism is fully realized. These sentiments aroused enthusiastic support from many young readers. Some critics, however, accused Zhang Jie of a 'petty-bourgeois mentality', of attacking the moral basis of society and of being unduly influenced by such western writers as Chekhov and Hardy. She also received anonymous letters accusing her of immorality because of her defence of love – even in the purest form – outside marriage, and because she is a divorcee.

Leaden Wings, published in 1980, is a novel which has as its central theme the modernization of Chinese industry. This is a topic of vital importance. For many years China's industrial growth was distorted and hampered by policies that paid too little attention to economic realities and were highly suspicious of allowing market forces much play. The results included unnecessarily low living standards for the people and appalling waste and inefficiency. Since the late 1970s a drastic reform programme has begun with the aim of bringing China's industry up to world standards, but at the time the novel is set it was facing formidable obstacles from officials who had made their careers under the old system.

In the Ministry of Heavy Industry are two opposing camps, the old guard and the reformists. There are officials concerned only with clinging to power; genuine followers of the ultra-Left line who believe that any other way of running industry except 'putting politics in command' is revisionist; men devoted to the people's interests, determined to end corruption and inefficiency; others who see the need for reform but are not prepared to stick their necks out to achieve it; and cynics who take no side, waiting to see who gains the upper hand.

In addition to the struggle between these officials, Zhang Jie presents junior members of the ministry, factory workers, the wives and children of the protagonists, and other peripheral characters. The story is open-ended, and it is tantalizing not to know what becomes of all the individuals who have aroused our interest. The aim of the novel, however, is not to tell their story but to give a picture of a society in a state of flux and to serve as a vehicle for Zhang Jie's views on the need for more democratic and scientific approaches, recognition of the value of the individual, understanding of the generation gap, and an overhauling of social morality by throwing out vestiges of feudalism.

Thus the inadequacy of the present marriage system is highlighted, this time mainly from the viewpoint of men. Out of six married couples described only one is happy. In China men hold power and are the ones who formulate moral values. Yet where love is concerned they too, if they want to retain their social positions, are victims of the ethics they themselves have created or condoned. Vice-minister Zheng has no love for the wife who has been unfaithful to him, yet in public he plays the part of a devoted husband in order not to spoil his political image. This hypocrisy is the main flaw in an otherwise admirable character dedicated to reform, and as a result his personal life is empty and meaningless. Fang, another advocate of modernization, when sent down to the countryside during the Cultural Revolution had fallen in love with a young widow after his wife had left him. He did not marry her though, thinking that once he was rehabilitated such a marriage would count against him; so he too has thrown away his chance of personal happiness. In accounts like these Zhang Jie makes clear her belief that men and women must together overthrow the outdated aspects of traditional moral values and establish genuine socialist ethics if they are to find fulfilment and happiness in their personal relations.

Zhang Jie is reflected in several characters, among them the uncompromising woman reporter Autumn, who tackles problems she is incapable of solving. But the author admits that the character who speaks most for her is Ho Jiabin, a minor official in the ministry whose unorthodox and outspoken views are used by his enemies to keep him out of the Party.

The publication of Leaden Wings sparked off conflicting reactions. Young people in industrial ministries commented that it painted a true picture. Some officials, outraged by Zhang Jie's barbed satire, accused her of making a slanderous attack on the Party and socialism. Her Party secretary called her in to answer their accusations. Zhang Jie denied the charges and insisted that she wrote this novel because she was a communist who supported socialism and the modernization of China.

With so many problems inherited from the past, so many man-made obstacles, will China's modernization programme succeed in rising on its leaden wings and soaring ahead to efficiency and affluence? Only the future can show. Zhang Jie is optimistic, putting her faith in the government's realistic policy and the efforts of China's millions.

'The Ark', her next major work, is about the difficulties of three divorcees trying to live independent and dignified lives in a man's world. It has been acclaimed as an original and important feminist novella. It has also been criticized on the grounds that the three central figures let their resentment against men embitter them and make them unwomanly.

Another of Zhang Jie's recent works, 'The Time Is Not Yet Ripe', won the National Best Story Award for 1984. Its theme is not unlike that of *Leaden Wings*. To facilitate China's modernization, elderly administrators are being required to retire and younger, abler men are being given leading posts. This story satirizes a bureaucratic Party secretary who schemes – but fails – to sabotage the promotion of a capable young engineer. Here again Zhang Jie expresses her conviction that in spite of all obstructions China's economy will forge ahead.

This translation of *Leaden Wings* is based on the version published in 1980 by the People's Literature Publishing House, which is rather long-winded and diffuse. In my opinion Chinese publishers do not do enough to encourage writers to compress and cut their work. Many of Zhang Jie's detailed descriptions and interior monologues are effective and subtle, giving fascinating insights into contemporary Chinese life and ways of thinking. But in places the arguments about politics and economic policy go on for far too long. The detailed accounts of procedure to streamline production, of behaviourism and the methods used by advanced countries to make industry more efficient, are skipped by most Chinese readers. As appreciation of these arguments requires an inside knowledge of the Chinese economy around 1980 they bear the main cuts that have been made with the author's permission.

Because so many characters appear in *Leaden Wings*, it is difficult for foreign readers to differentiate between their names. In general these are written according to the Chinese phonetic alphabet; but I have changed the surname 'He' to 'Ho' to avoid confusion with the pronoun 'he'. I have also given some of the main women characters English names.

Finally I would like to thank Bill Jenner who spent his spare time in the sweltering Beijing summer improving my translation and Delia Davin who polished it once more, arranged its publication and checked the proofs for me.

Gladys Yang, Beijing, 1986

Our salvation lies in this simple saying of an ordinary individual: Practice is the sole criterion of truth.

1

An appetizing smell of beetroot soup came wafting from the kitchen, with it the rhythmic sound of chopping.

Perhaps because Ye Zhiqiu – Autumn – had got over her illness, her heart felt light on this fine winter day. She felt as if she had recovered the appetite she once had as a student, when she could wolf down five ounces of rice at one meal. She was in a mood to play some prank out of keeping with her age.

But of course she mustn't; her hair was turning grey. Even at home she had to watch her step, because if she let herself go there and it became a habit, she might do the same in her office or in public, scandalizing everyone. As it was, though she tried to hold herself in check, some people considered her a ridiculous misfit because of her inadvertent carelessness. Heavens! She was just the simplest of beings. But since the ten years of turmoil, the more complex or fantastic anything was, the more normal and rational it seemed to people. Simple, truthful statements struck them as abnormal and difficult to understand. She was over forty now, yet still had not learned how to cope with life.

So she tried to repress her elation, to behave like a middle-aged Chinese woman. Perhaps she didn't try hard enough, for a little of it came bubbling out as she called in her rusty French, 'Qu'est-ce qu'on mange au déjeuner?'

Mo Zheng promptly called back from the kitchen, 'De la soupe au potiron, de saucisson et du pain.'

Good lad, he hadn't forgotten his French. That came of his upbringing in a cultured family.

1

A cultured family? But now he had nothing. Like her he was an orphan.

Once, sure enough, he had a warm, cultured home.

But what was culture? For some years it had been an intolerable luxury, a synonym for 'bourgeois'.

What fools human beings were to have created material civilization. If they had stayed as they were at the time of the flood, life would have been much simpler.

Mo Zheng's parents had taught French at a top university. During the fifties Autumn had been their student. Mo Zheng had only been three then, an adorable child dressed in light blue flannel who reminded her of little Oliver Twist in the English film. His black eyes had flashed like gems. Before every meal he would wash his hands and put them on the table to show his mama, then ask respectfully, 'Est-ce que je peux manger?' Whenever Autumn called on Professor Mo, she would tease the child by calling him Oliver. Her joke had later turned into a witch's curse, and like Oliver Twist he had ended up an orphan.

It wasn't just that he was destitute. Life had robbed him of his birthright and forced things on him that he should never have known. After his parents were killed in the Cultural Revolution the boy had roamed the streets like a homeless cur, living on what he could steal. The first time that Autumn had fetched him home from the police station, he had savagely bitten her hand. How could a vagrant, who only knew hands stretched out to hit him, conceive of a helping hand?

Autumn had fetched him back from the police station again, not even aware herself why she did so.

Perhaps it was because she too had been an orphan, had suffered the pain of living in a home that was not her own. This pain created a bond between them.

Perhaps it was because she knew she would never have any other outlet for her maternal love.

Nothing is more agonizing for a woman than ugliness.

There was nothing grotesque about any of Autumn's features, but taken together they made her one of the ugliest women alive. Her hair, in keeping with her character, was a thick, wiry mane. It looked old-fashioned too, as she refused to have it thinned out or styled. It stuck out in all directions, and from a distance looked like a soldier's helmet.

She had no feminine curves or charm either. Her square shoulders were like a tree stump hewn with an axe.

No man in his right senses would marry such a woman.

The strongest characters may be the weakest. Always prepared to be trampled upon or destroyed, in the end they grow callous and cold. Then nothing has greater power over them than warmth, for having received so little of it they treasure it. And Autumn had treated Mo Zheng not simply with warmth but with a mother's love. The two of them were probably happier together than people in most normal families, but that was not understood by such people.

Lunch was brought in.

Like an experienced waiter, Mo Zheng held two steaming bowls of soup in his right hand, two plates of bread and sausage in his left. On each plate was also a tiny dab of jam. The fine slices of sausage were laid out in a circle. The neatly cut slices of bread might have been measured with a ruler.

Each time she watched Mo Zheng preparing a meal so efficiently in the kitchen, a faint mysterious smile on his face as he scraped the scoop on the bottom of the pan, Autumn's feelings were mixed. He seemed better equipped to survive than her generation. For instance, she still couldn't cook. But for him, she would be reduced to eating in the canteen where everything tasted the same. She liked tasty food but begrudged spending time on cooking. Her life was too disorganized. She often thought that Mo Zheng could make a success of anything he turned his hand to, whether cooking, playing the piano or learning French.

The soup was so hot that, after putting it down, Mo Zheng blew on the tips of his fingers. He had the hands of an artist: long fingers, broad, thick palms, strong knuckles and wrists. He had played the piano for several years as a child, when he was still too small to reach the pedals,

3

forgetting his food and games as he pounded away. Now, however, whenever she felt the urge to play the dusty piano with her stiff, refractory fingers, he would retreat to a corner of his room as if afraid of the sound.

Mo Zheng was no longer the little boy in light blue flannel. He was a tall young man in a crumpled and padded PLA jacket from an army surplus sale. He had replaced the original buttons with five of different sizes and colours. The cuffs of his long baggy trousers were usually torn, as his job was pruning, watering and spraying trees and shrubs. Even so, girls who didn't know his history were attracted by his square jaw, full lips, soft hair parted in the middle and combed loosely back, and arching eyebrows the tips of which curved down, so that even when still he struck people as animated. The pupils of his eyes were unusually large, and he would look slowly around, seriously and coolly. This contrast between his eyebrows and his eyes was what made his face so striking.

With one foot Mo Zheng hooked out a stool from under the table. It creaked when he sat on it, as if unable to bear his weight.

That creaking worried Autumn. Time and again she had urged him to take the stool to be repaired before it collapsed and somebody got hurt. Be he always shrugged this off. 'It's nothing. Just remember not to sit on it yourself!' It wasn't that he was lazy, but to him a fall was nothing to worry about. She had to let it go at that, but she couldn't help eyeing the stool each time it creaked.

Now he asked as if casually, 'Well? Do you like the flavour?'

Autumn blew on a spoonful of soup, then tasted it. She smiled. 'Not bad. The real thing – like your French accent.'

Mo Zheng's spoon stopped in mid air. Why did she have to rake up the past? He disliked recalling it, yet could never free himself from it. He gulped down a spoonful of soup as if to swallow his own anger. Then with his strong white teeth he bit into a slice of bread.

There was a crash, and for a second she thought his stool

had collapsed. But no, the sound came from upstairs. Something must have been knocked over. Then they heard Little Zhuang howling, heavy footfalls and his mother Liu Yuyin — Jade — sobbing.

Mo Zheng smiled rather grimly. 'Like people out of Gorki.'

Autumn stopped eating.

'What's wrong?' he asked, still smiling faintly.

She looked sheepish. The wordly-wise, phlegmatic Mo Zheng made her feel like an ingenuous little girl, too easily upset. 'I don't know why, but I can't eat when I hear crying.'

'Like a real Christian.'

'Mo Zheng!' she protested, feeling he could see through her. She stood up to go out. He barred the way with one of his long legs. 'Take it easy! What can you do about it? They'll be rowing again within a couple of days.'

He was right. The children upstairs were always crying and their parents always quarrelling. They were not a cantankerous couple and the two children were well-behaved, so why was life getting them down?

Mo Zheng urged her to finish her soup before it got cold, but Autumn's appetite had gone, along with her earlier high spirits. She shook her head.

She sat down silently at her desk and leafed through the last few days' papers. She noted, as always, which new factories had started production, which enterprises had over-fulfilled their quotas. These reports reminded her that the year was drawing to an end. In just over a month it would be 1980. At once she remembered the article she had been about to write before her illness, and started looking for her draft of it.

Strange, where had it gone? She distinctly remembered putting it on this pile of documents. It wasn't there. Had she slipped it into a drawer?

She opened her drawers one by one. Every one was a mess. Diaries, stationery, old letters, stamps, envelopes of money, empty medicine bottles. . . all lay in complete confusion. And she lacked the patience to make a careful search. She tossed an empty bottle into a corner.

She could not bring herself to throw away those old letters. Although not from friends, they were a record of her life, of her gallant failures.

She was a reporter who sympathized with the victims of injustice and waxed indignant over all abuses of which there had been so many in recent years. The ordinary workers and grassroot cadres whom she interviewed trusted her. She had overreached herself intervening in problems which were none of her business and often failed to solve them. These letters had made her feel guilty, as if she had deceived those good, honest people, yet they still looked to her for help. It was hard. Visitors from far away would turn up on her doorstep, rubbing their big-jointed hands, smiling bashfully and looking rather red in the face, then pour out their grievances till the middle of the night. Mo Zheng's room was like an inn.

The last couple of years had seen a marked change in her correspondence. She had received letters from families who had been cleared, whose sons, formerly excluded by people with pull, had now got into college; from people once labelled as renegades but now rehabilitated; from others no longer persecuted because the Party secretaries who had risen to power by joining some clique had now been dismissed. She hadn't the heart to throw away such letters.

But she had to find that draft.

'Mo Zheng, did you see a sheet of paper on my desk?' She knew it was useless to tell him it was a draft: the boy thought so little of her job, he never read what she wrote.

'What paper?'

'A sheet of lined paper with writing on it.'

'Oh, when Little Zhuang came here to play the day before yesterday I wrapped some sweets up for him in a sheet of waste paper from your desk.'

'That wasn't waste paper, it was the draft of a report I'm writing on this year's industrial output.'

'How was I to know?' He didn't sound at all contrite.

6

'I've told you often enough not to touch my writing! You pay not a blind bit of notice.'

Mo Zheng looked sorry now. Not for tearing up her draft, but for upsetting her. He said, 'But what's the hurry? You need a good rest. Besides, who reads those reports with all that pompous official nonsense? Who believes them?'

'What a thing to say! Your ideas are getting wilder and wilder.' She pounded the desk.

Mo Zheng kept quiet and went on eating. The only sounds in the room were the clinks of his spoon against the bowl and his soft munching.

In their frequent clashes he was usually the one who backed down, not wanting to upset her. She was the only person in the world who loved him, who didn't hold his past against him. Anyhow, he thought his generation superior to hers.

He could not grasp why, with only twenty years between their ages, there was such an amazing difference in their understanding of life. Were all her generation like her? More or less. In their purity of heart and credulity they clung stubbornly to their obsolete ideas.

Their arguments often rankled in Autumn's mind. She didn't consider herself a brainless woman. She had original ideas and keen insight. It was only his generation who thought all older people fuddy-duddies.

She had worked as a reporter for twenty-odd years since graduating from college in 1956, coming into touch with all sorts of people and getting a good grasp of the way things really were. She had her own views, and had resolved never to write false reports. In the Cultural Revolution she had found excuses for writing nothing rather than joining the chorus of those dishonest theoreticians.

She knew a lot of people working in industry. It comforted her to find that there were still some doing an honest job. And she loved to collect figures of increased output, which were not just dry statistics to her. She threw herself whole-heartedly into her work. How could Mo Zheng malign it like that?

7

Her jaw quivering with anger, she glared at him and stamped her foot.

Mo Zheng stopped eating, realizing that she had misunderstood him. He wiped the faint smile off his face and said seriously, 'I wasn't talking about your work but about those endless statistics. Some people imagine they're sent up from below, worked out by abacus. In fact there's nothing that can't be faked, including Chairman Mao's "supreme instructions". The papers always claim that our industrial output is going up. Rubbish! I'm not saying all those figures are false, but I see no point in them. Take Old Wu upstairs. How does his family manage? Someone ought to write a truthful report on how the workers who sweat to create society's wealth live. That would show whether our industry has really developed. What use are your statistics? Have you ever thought about that?' For once Mo Zheng had lost his temper. He shoved his bowl aside so that the soup slopped on to his trousers. Then he pulled out a dirty, crumpled handkerchief to mop his trouser legs and work off his feelings.

Slowly her resentment died down. There was some sense in what he said, immature though it was. She thought bitterly of the mistakes, the chops and changes in the economic policy since 1956. But for all that the people would surely have a higher standard of living. Still, they were better off than before Liberation.

She said feebly, 'At least these figures show that our economy has grown every year. Compared with before Liberation. . .'

'I knew you'd say that,' he cut in. 'You can't go on making that comparison for ever. How can you compare the old days with socialism?' Unwilling to carry on with the argument, he chucked his handkerchief into what was left of the soup, and sprang up to clear the table. At the kitchen door he turned, and it seemed as if a gust of wind had blown the dark clouds off his face. 'You really ought to think about Old Wu's family, and why they keep having rows.'

She felt the force of his sincerity. He seldom showed

8

warmth, thinking tender-heartedness a weakness in a man, a luxury that he could not afford, was not fool enough to expect. . .

But no matter how cold-hearted he tried to appear he was filled with genuine feeling, selflessness and aspirations. Old Wu's family had been their neighbours for years. Autumn remembered how devoted he had been to his wife Jade. During Jade's first pregnancy everyone in the building had teased him for the way he cosseted her. Granny Wang on the second floor used to say, 'Don't worry, Young Wu. Having a baby is like a hen laying an egg. If you get so worked up you'll scare her.' Still he looked after his wife very carefully. Jade had been a charming bride and he had been a handsome young man, yet in a dozen years things had changed completely. Wu Guodong was so rough now, balding prematurely, and his wife's forehead was lined.

2

Not bad at all, this perm, just what Xia Zhuyun – Bamboo – had wanted. Really stylish. At her age it wouldn't do to wear her hair in tight curls like a girl. That looked vulgar, cheap, as if you could only afford a perm once a year.

She surveyed herself complacently in the two mirrors. Then standing up she nodded at Jade who was holding the mirror behind.

Bamboo thought: She knows her job, no wonder she was recommended to me. But why does she look so unhappy? She's still young. What's on her mind?

She relaxed as she waited for her handbag and coat.

It was a thick, dark grey coat, yet very light, made of good worsted. The handbag was special too, flat and wide with an embossed design, a gift from her husband after his last visit to England.

Wherever he went on business, he always brought her back a present. Then she would smile like an empress receiving tribute.

Jade stood watching as Bamboo slowly put on her coat and headscarf, taking care not to spoil her new hairdo, then slowly opened her handbag. Her slowness was not deliberate but second nature. For, this middle-aged wife of a highly-placed official had lived in affluence for years, accustomed to being waited on by others.

From her handbag Bamboo took out an elegant leather purse with two gold-coloured metal clasps. In it were half a dozen ten-yuan notes, as much if not more than Jade's monthly salary.

Bamboo extracted one note and twisted it between her thumb and first finger before handing it over.

Jade took it up to the counter. At the sight of her worried, careworn face, Little Gu glanced at the clock. 'Half-past five, time for you to knock off.'

Jade smiled at her for her kind thought, but remembered the troubles waiting for her at home.

The notes in the change were dirty and crumpled. Bamboo took them superciliously, but didn't forget to count them before she clicked her purse shut.

She left, glancing at her small gold wristwatch. The perm had taken nearly four hours. That did not worry her; her problem was how to kill time. Her maid saw to all the laundry, cleaning and cooking. Their only daughter still at home was grown-up and had a very good job as a press photographer. Her sole worry was how to find the girl a suitable husband.

When she felt so inclined she would go to her office. If her heart was troubling her she rested at home. But she couldn't spend the whole day sleeping. Knitting helped to pass the time, though she never finished anything. And of course she could always read. They subscribed to many magazines and papers, and she spent hours reading. Unlike so many wives of high officials she had graduated from university, but her affluent life had corroded her mental faculties. Whatever she read she forgot.

10

In the evenings her husband had meetings and her daughter went out, so she sat alone on a sofa watching their twenty-inch Japanese colour TV. She often closed her eyes and dozed off, so that when she went to bed she couldn't sleep and had to find something to occupy her mind. Often she thought about her daughter's marriage. Deputy-commander Wang's second son wasn't engaged, but he was too feeble and had no real talent. Ambassador Yu's son was sickly – she didn't want her daughter to be an early widow. Minister Tian's third son wasn't bad-looking and was bright, he worked as a translator, but perhaps he already had a girl friend?. . . Sometimes she got up to knock on her husband's door, but he never opened it, either because he was sound asleep or because he knew that it was never anything that mattered.

Of course, at her age she didn't spend all that time on her appearance to make herself attractive; she just wanted to be smart, in keeping with her status. Her husband, busy with endless meetings, visits to the grass roots or telephone calls, had no time to admire her clothes or her hair-styles.

Once in 1956 she had dragged him to a dance in Beijing Hotel. The next day she asked, 'Did it suit me, that dress I wore yesterday?'

He thought hard. 'Not bad. Yellow goes well with your complexion.'

Bamboo gaped at him. 'What! Are you colour-blind? I was wearing a purple silk gown!'

He roared with laughter. 'Well, why not get yourself a yellow one made?' Yet when she had a yellow silk dress made he said, 'Yellow? Doesn't suit you.'

Apart from this she had no complaints about him. He had been such a handsome, dashing young man that many girls had envied her when they went out together. He had never shown any interest in other women. In fact he treated even her as an ornament he could easily dispense with. They had long slept in separate rooms. She wondered if he regretted having married. Had he ever really loved her? He immersed himself so thoroughly in his work that his home and two daughters seemed to mean nothing to him. If she hadn't pulled strings their younger girl would never have found such an ideal job. It carried a high status but wasn't strenuous, and it brought her in touch with all sorts of important people. Of course she would have to fix up a good flat for her family too. When her husband regained his old post the ministry's housing shortage had forced them to accept this flat. A vice-minister deserved something better than five rooms on the third floor. Especially since she had a weak heart and her old man had asthma. She'd have to see it it, he wouldn't do a thing.

When Bamboo left the hairdresser's Jade felt completely limp. She hadn't slept a wink last night, had left home without breakfast and had been too upset to eat lunch. She didn't want to sit down and rest, though. She had to find something to do to keep from crying. She started sweeping the floor.

Her parents had never spanked or scolded her. But yesterday she'd been struck by her husband for whom she would have laid down her life. Why? All because Little Zhuang had broken a thermos flask. Wu Guodong had slapped the child without even asking if he had scalded himself. All she'd said was, 'A flask only costs one yuan. What did you have to hit him for?'

'You're talking like a minister's wife,' he had retorted. 'How many one yuan do you have?'

It was true: towards the end of the month she had to count every cent.

Since Wu had gone on sick leave with hepatitis he drew only sixty per cent of his monthly pay, just over forty yuan, while she made fifty at most. Four mouths to feed, and every month they had to send his parents fifteen yuan. He needed nourishing food too, and they couldn't let the children go without.

There were others even worse off, and they could just make ends meet, but Jade had her work cut out to manage.

To save a few cents she never bought ready-made noodles.

She kneaded dough and cut her own, even though her ankles were swollen after standing in the shop all day.

She never bought fresh vegetables, only the cheap ones that were sold off at ten cents a pile. Her elder sister wrote from Xinjiang* that greens were expensive there. Beijing was better – you could always find cut-price things.

To economize on detergent, she washed light-coloured clothes first, then dark ones, then the two boys' shoes,** and finally the mop.

Things had been different when she was a girl. She looked back wistfully on the years before 1958 when everyone had been better off. And since 1965 things had gone from bad to worse.

She hid her hardships from her parents, not wanting to worry them as they weren't having an easy time themselves. Her dad had retired, and her younger brother now had a baby daughter. Each time she went to see them, Jade spruced up the kids and took a box of cheap cakes. This didn't fool her mother. On the boys' birthdays or at festivals she helped her daughter out with a little money in ways which wouldn't hurt her son-in-law's pride.

A few days ago Jade had been going to make a winter jacket, and some beige dacron took her fancy. But it would have cost over ten yuan. She hestitated for a while by the counter, then bought some cotton instead. Better save the money to buy Guodong some nourishing food. And the boys both needed new padded shoes.

She spared no pains yet received not a word of thanks. Instead her husband swore at her and took things out on their sons even when they had done nothing wrong. In her resentment she had snapped at him, 'Why aren't you a minister?'

'Why didn't you marry one?'

Neither would back down, each felt so wronged. They went for each other hammer and tongs. And when Jade tried to stop him hitting Little Zhuang, he had slapped her

* A border province in north-west China.
** Chinese cloth shoes.

in the face. The next moment he stood aghast at his own behaviour.

Jade hadn't cried, but just stared at him steadily, as if only now, after all these years, had she realized what he was really like.

They had often had rows before but this was the first time they had ever come to blows. Who was to blame?

That slap had brought Wu to his senses and made him realize that Jade was the mainstay of the family. Without her they could never have kept going. Had he ever asked her how she managed on so little money? No. Had he shown any concern for her? No. She had taken the heavy burden on her weak shoulders without a word of complaint.

Perhaps women are tougher and more self-sacrificing than men.

But he had not been able to bring himself to apologize. Perhaps it was because an apology would not have been enough. It might have made her even angrier.

In that instant Jade had thought, why not die and be done with it? Let him regret it for the rest of his life. But then who would look after the children? They might have a cruel stepmother. The thought made her weep. No, she could not die. What about a divorce? No, people would think she'd done something disgraceful. Divorcees were always despised, talked about behind their backs. And she couldn't go home to her mother: they had no room for her. Besides, that would only worry the old couple. . . She had been wondering all day how to punish her husband.

Why was fate so cruel to her? What a different life that last customer must have. Her husband would never beat her or say a harsh word.

She brushed away the tears with the back of her hand before anyone could see them.

It was snowing. Fluffy white snowflakes swirled gaily in the wind – the first snowfall this year. They reminded her of her happy girlhood.

A young man and a girl came in. The cold wind had brought colour to the girl's cheeks and made her eyes

14

sparkle. The young man was carrying two big shopping-bags stuffed with purchases. He stood there beaming.

Jade sized them up at once as a couple about to get married.

The girl said, 'Comrade, I'm looking for a hairdresser named Liu. . .'

'What for?'

The young man cleared his throat, as if to stress the importance of his statement: 'We want her to do a perm. People say she's very good.'

'Any of our stylists can give you a good perm,' Little Gu put in. She thought Jade needed a rest. She was too kind-hearted to refuse if asked for by name.

The young man looked flummoxed. This was the first time in his life he had tried to do anything like this. Couldn't they grasp how important it was to him and his bride-to-be?

Jade understood. To him, his fiancée mattered more than anything else on earth. Tired out and wretched as she was, she felt touched.

'I'm Liu,' she admitted.

'All right then,' Little Gu sighed. 'I'll give you a ticket for her.' She whispered reproachfully to Jade, 'Your face is swollen.'

The girl handed over some notes. 'A cold perm.'

Little Gu pushed the money back looking at the clock. 'It's too late for a cold perm.'

The young couple stared at each other in dismay.

'I shan't have any time tomorrow,' said the girl.

Jade glanced at Little Gu, who relented: 'Very well. Liu's doing you a great favour.'

The girl looked at the photographs of different hair styles, then asked her fiancé, 'Which would suit me best?'

'Ask the stylist,' he suggested.

Jade said, 'All right, leave it to me.' Just about to cut off the girl's plaits, she glanced at the young man and saw mixed feelings in his eyes. 'Would you prefer to cut them off yourself?' she asked.

It came as a surprise to them, the intuition of this middle-aged woman with her lined, swollen face. No wonder people spoke so well of her.

The young man took the scissors, cut off the plaits, looked at them for a long time, then put them carefully into a small plastic bag. He reminded Jade of her husband years ago.

Jade gave the final touches to the girl's hair with the drier. The mirror reflected two very different faces. Next to that rosy face with sparkling eyes, Jade looked old and washed out. She thought, 'I hope you'll always look as fresh and lovely.'

The girl gazed bashfully at her unfamiliar reflection, the waved hair giving her the look of a young married woman. She smiled shyly.

The two young people somehow felt that everything, commonplace though it might be, that happened here on the eve of their wedding, including their meeting this commonplace hairdresser, would influence the whole of their married life.

In a flurry the young man produced a paper bag and handed it to Jade. 'Please take some of our wedding sweets!'

'I couldn't,' said Jade. 'But thank you all the same.'

When he insisted, she took out two sweets. They were wrapped in red paper with the character for 'Double Happiness'. She then thrust the rest back into his shopping-bag and saw them out.

There were few people in the snow-covered street. Jade stood and watched the happy young couple walking away.

When they had disappeared from sight she turned and suddenly saw her husband leaning against a nearby tree. He must have been there for some time: his old padded cap, shoulders and scarf were white with snow. Clutching the sweets she watched him come over to her.

3

Ho Jiabin looked sternly at the fat, greasy face before him. His visitor was fairly young, but years of over-eating and drinking had left accumulations of fat on his sagging cheeks, jowls and stomach.

Ho thought, 'Worried, are you? Serve you right! May help you lose some weight.'

Actually the fellow was not as worried as he made out. A purchasing agent who travelled all over the country, he had learned the right face to put on for different people. Ho Jiabin should be easy to cope with. He must butter him up. If that failed he could bypass the fellow and go straight to Director Feng, an old comrade-in-arms of his Party secretary who had opened the back door to supply the equipment for their power plant. His present request was not exorbitant, but you couldn't keep troubling a director over the least little thing. You had to make the best use of connections and strike while the iron was hot. Connections were like money in the bank which should be used in emergencies but replenished from time to time.

He said with an ingratiating smile, 'Can I trouble you to remind the factory to downgrade the volt meter. We hadn't time to see to it when we made out the order.'

'Rubbish. You must have known when you filled out the order. Or were your people drunk at the time?' Ho pounded the crumpled order form on his desk. 'Anyhow, it's nothing to do with me. Your plant isn't in the state plan, so you've no right to get equipment from us. How the devil did you wangle that?'

Ho Jiabin was working off his anger. He knew that the man confronting him had been a shop assistant in a county town. He might have been good at that, though he looked so greasy and corrupt; but now he had landed a job as purchasing agent. Because he was the brother-in-law of the power plant's head he could get away with squandering public money.

Their plant was only a small one, yet in 1975 a certain leading official had let them install a 125,000 kilowatt set of generators, because the man in charge of building it had once been his bodyguard. Ho had been in the Ministry of Heavy Industry for many a long year, and ever since the start of the Cultural Revolution he had seen any number of plants set up just on the word of some big shot, regardless of whether or not they were in the state plan. Who took the plan seriously? That could always be changed. Then every year they complained of over-extended construction. Of course, anybody who pleased could add new projects. But if five people's rations were shared among ten, everyone went short. Yet this was justified as 'share and share alike'.

But it was so hard to cut back on construction. Each project had powerful backing. So they muddled along at a snail's pace. It was nothing unusual for a project to take ten years to complete. But no one worried, because no one's personal interests were affected.

This purchasing agent knew a trick or two. Not long ago he had delivered loads of cut-price walnuts, dates, eggs and good bamboo-leaf liqueur for everyone in the ministry to share. Naturally these things, unobtainable outside, were paid for, so no one refused them. Besides, they were dirt cheap.

Here in the ministry they lacked for nothing. Day lilies, edible fungus, peanuts, ginseng. . . Every province had to build power plants and each had its own local products. The power people could get anything they wanted in their areas. If you didn't cough up they cut off your power. But whoever wanted equipment for new plants had to keep in with the distributors. It was always easier to do business with friends, who could tip the balance in your favour when a decision was evenly balanced.

It was like a tumour on some vital organ. If you cut it off that would endanger your life, so fresh blood kept circulating through the tumour to nourish its redundant cells till it burst.

Ho had heard that this small power plant had sent half a dozen men to Beijing to get extra state funds and buy material and equipment. They had taken a room in a hostel for several months and went everywhere by taxi – paid for by the peasants' blood and sweat. If they were competent it wouldn't be so bad. But they couldn't even fill in an order card properly. He snorted bitterly.

Of course, Ho knew it was no use losing his temper like a child. He was nearing fifty, had worked for over twenty years, yet still remained such a stickler for the correct procedure. But he couldn't even control something like this. The crook could approach Director Feng, who could ask Section Chief Li to find someone smart like Old Shi to see to it. Shi Quanqing was only too glad of chances like this, and would self-righteously claim that building this plant would be helping to modernize agriculture. He was for ever reporting on his work to Director Feng, as he wanted to join the Party.

Shi was unobtrusively keeping tabs on Ho. Right now he appeared absorbed in the daily summary of the world press the government puts out for officials, but his ears were flapping. He never missed a word of what was said.

Shi thought Ho ridiculously naive. In all their years as colleagues he had seen Ho come a cropper several times. Each time he gloated. So he stored this confrontation away in his mind for future use.

The door of the office opened and Section Chief Li – Grace – made her entrance. She looked upset so Shi guessed that she had business with Ho.

She realized from Shi's sympathetic yet indignant expression that Ho had been reprimanding a 'comrade from a grass-roots unit'.

Grace pulled a still longer face and knitted her short eyebrows.

She walked to Ho's desk, paused for effect, and was just about to speak when the telephone rang.

It was a long-distance call.

Ho picked up the receiver. 'Hullo. Who's there?'

'A long-distance call for Ho Jiabin.'

'This is Ho Jiabin speaking.'

'Hullo, is that Ho? I'm Cai from the Taohua Hydro-electric Station.'

'What do you want?'

'Well. . . Well. . .'

'Stop welling. Out with it! What's wrong? This is a long-distance call. Every minute costs money.'

'It's like this, we ordered a hydraulic turbine from Austria. . .'

'I know.'

'They've just sent us the technical specifications. A lot of the equipment we ordered from you last time isn't up to these specifications. We want to cancel some of the order.'

Cai had a nerve. He didn't even sound apologetic. 'I told you, didn't I, to wait for the technical data before ordering accessories!' Ho bellowed. 'The factory's already started production. You can't cancel now.'

'It wasn't our fault. Our superiors told us to place the orders with you, so as not to hold up the project. And it was all above-board, in line with the state plan.'

Normally with new construction projects strict procedures had to be followed. Blueprints and all the specifications of the main equipment and accessories had to be sent in before it could be included in the state plan. But in the summer three places in the provinces under Ho's charge had ordered equipment for power plants without supplying the necessary data – one had not even decided on a site or what fuel to use.

'Who'll be responsible for the losses?' demanded Ho. A stupid question. No one would be responsible. 'Will you compensate the factory for its loss?'

Crafty Old Cai promptly promised, 'Yes, we will.'

'You can't simply cancel your order. You'll have to give us a written explanation for us to pass on to the factory.'

'All right.'

Ho rang off, making a mental note to write to the State Council about this sort of confusion. All problems dating from before the fall of the Gang of Four could be blamed on them. But now that they had gone, if the present chaos in construction was allowed to continue, how could limited resources be put to best use and waste cut out? How could there even be talk of speeding up China's modernization?

As he mopped his perspiring forehead, Grace tapped his desk impatiently. Only then did he turn his thoughts from economic problems and realize that she wanted to talk to him. He knew she had a low opinion of him. If he asked what she wanted she would probably bite his head off.

'Your section chief tells me you haven't yet handed in your personal summary of what you've learned from Daqing.'*

'I told you I've no intention of writing one.'

Grace assumed the look of a judge passing sentence. 'Very well then, Director Feng would like to see you.'

The man with the greasy face smiled spitefully.

Shi lowered his eyes to hide his satisfaction. It was curious, Ho had never offended Shi, yet Shi detested him. Their characters were incompatible.

Grace had got on well enough with Ho till the re-election last year of the Party committee. Guo Hongcai really wasn't up to handling propaganda, so on the surface it was reasonable for Grace's candidate Luo to replace him. But the real reason Grace had it in for Guo was because he kept making trouble for her in branch committee meetings. For instance, when she and Luo had sponsored Shi to join the Party, they'd by-passed their branch as most of its members disapproved and sent Shi's application straight up to the bureau committee. Guo had protested about this to Commissioner Fang, who had sent for her and given her, as branch secretary, a dressing-down. And that wasn't the only time they'd clashed. So she and Luo had been looking for ways to do Guo down, but they could find nothing against him. With disunity in the Party branch, non-Party people in the section had also split into two factions. Ho

* A successful oilfield in north-east China held up as an example to industry in the 1960s and 1970s. There were many campaigns for industrial units to 'learn from Daqing'.

Jiabin and others had criticized her more than once for this and urged her to call a meeting to thrash matters out.

Finally Grace had convened a meeting. Luo was always complaining about Guo to her, but on this occasion he had said not a word. When they split up for small-group discussion, however, he had held forth non-stop. Ho Jiabin frowned, and Shi said, 'Watch your tongue. Someone may report what you say. It would be seen as undermining unity.'

That had goaded Ho to put in, 'Why not say all this to Comrade Guo's face instead of running him down behind his back? Who's undermining unity?'

'I didn't mean you,' said Shi.

Grace's face had been black. 'We're talking to the whole section, not running someone down behind his back.'

'Oh yes you are. As a Party member and the section chief you shouldn't let Shi slander Guo, let alone side with him. I refuse to stay in this meeting.' He stood up and left.

Word of this soon spread, but it was none of Ho's doing. When the bureau Party committee learned of this clash, Director Feng had sent for Ho and a few others to discuss it.

However, Feng had later told Grace all they had said. This only made matters worse. It had ended with Grace making Ho and other critics of hers study Chairman Mao's essay on liberalism for a week. *

There was something rather intimidating about the closed door of Room 213, where so many people's fates were decided. This was the office that appointed section chiefs and decided on salary increases, promotions, admissions to the Party and transfers.

On the way to Room 213, Ho thought of applying for a transfer. But what else could he do? He was nearly fifty and had spent over twenty years in this ministry without achieving anything. He had studied physics at university,

---

* Mao Zedong wrote a famous attack on unprincipled behaviour, entitled 'Combat Liberalism'.

and if he had been given a suitable job then he might have done something useful. But he had not kept up with new developments in physics, and had virtually forgotten the little he once knew. He had frittered away his life.

'Director Feng, you sent for me?'

Feng raised his massive head, the head of a thinker. Perhaps his mind was still on the document in front of him as he stared blankly at Ho. 'I sent for you? . . . Oh, that's right. I wanted to talk to you. Sit down.'

Feng settled himself more comfortably in his chair, took off his old-fashioned glasses and fiddled with them.

Feng still dressed much as he had when he first came to Beijing with the army. He still wore the black cloth shoes of the ordinary people. In summer he liked to unbutton his shirt and roll his vest up to his armpits, rubbing his chest as if soaping himself in a bath, or he might roll up his trousers to massage his hairy legs. In winter he took off his shoes and kneaded his toes. All this was a conditioned reflex during meetings. When not in meetings or talking he gave an impression of depth and inscrutability as now. Ho could not tell whether the director was weighing his words or whether he had simply forgotten why he had sent for him.

Feng was in fact reviewing his impressions of Ho in order to decide what tone to adopt. Ho was not a model in learning from Daqing, nor an advanced worker. He was too fond of making biting criticisms, held some weird views and argued for the sake of arguing. He was quite a theoretician, for ever quoting Marx and Engels. And when Feng had been sent the local products from his old home Ho had reported him to Commissioner Fang. Feng had got Grace to settle that by explaining that these gifts were an expression of thanks and should of course be shared by everyone. As he himself lacked for nothing, he had declared stoutly that he did not want any. Later Grace had delivered some of the walnuts and bamboo-leaf liqueur to his home, and he had paid much less than the market price. But Grace had been careless and word of this had got out. Fang had seized on it at a Party meeting to warn against accepting gifts from units not in the state plan, then allotting them supplies. He'd really made a mountain out of a mole-hill!

Feng knew he couldn't afford a head-on clash with Fang. In each confrontation he played stupid. He would have his revenge one day, for being in charge of personnel he had surrounded the commissioner with his own people, who kept him informed of all Fang said and did.

What had Old Fang ever really done in all his years working for the revolution? He had joined it in 1941, two years later than Feng, and finally become a commissioner. How? Because he had a bit more education. Well, education often led people astray.

It suddenly occurred to him that Old Fang had a lot in common with Ho Jiabin. Feng decided to use devious tactics.

'How are you getting on these days?'

'What do you mean?'

Feng frowned. What sort of answer was that? Had the fellow no respect for the leadership? But not wanting to antagonize him he said patiently, 'In your thinking, work and life.'

Ho guessed that this had something to do with his refusal to summarize what he had learned from Daqing. But he wasn't going to bring this up himself. He answered vaguely, 'Things are going all right.'

'That's not good enough. Our bureau aims at becoming a Daqing-type unit within two years. That means each of us must work in the Daqing style.'

Here we go! thought Ho.

'What's your personal Daqing plan?'

'I haven't made one.'

'Why not? This is a question of principle.'

'That's not how I see it.' Ho chuckled inwardly, wondering if Feng knew how many people in the ministry had just copied these so-called personal plans from each other.

Feng put on his spectacles and stared at Ho as if he were some strange animal in the zoo. Should he pin a label on him? No, the time for that had passed, and it was no longer taken seriously.

24

Criticize him then? But how? His attitude to Daqing was outrageous. Daqing was a red banner that Chairman Mao had raised, and here was one of his subordinates opposing it. If word of this got out, it would reflect badly on Feng. He decided to make his own attitude clear.

'I think you're completely mistaken. Your view is dangerous!'

'I haven't expressed any view.'

Trust an intellectual to talk back. But Feng could outsmart him.

'Let's hear your view then. Why won't you make a plan and write a summary?'

'The sister of a friend of mine works in an oil production crew in Daqing. I met her last time she came home and asked her what she did in her spare time.

'"Nothing," she told me.

'"Don't you read novels?" I asked.

'"No."

'"See films?"

'"No."

'"Read the papers?"

'"No."

'That staggered me. "Then how do you spend your time off?" I asked.

'"We don't have any except Saturday evenings. All the other evenings we have political study, then wash and go to bed. We've only recently got a bathhouse."

'I ask you. Do you think those girls don't want to keep abreast of events, take an interest in what's going on in the world, or better themselves? Of course they do. But they simply haven't the energy. We talk about surpassing the United States and the Soviet Union. Their oil crews have much lighter work than ours. We've got to mechanize and modernize if we're to outstrip them. Of course our workers know where their duty lies, and when the going's tough they can take it. But we shouldn't squander their efforts. They need time to master the technology if they're to operate sophisticated equipment. Don't you realize that

25

those girls want love and babies too. . . they're human beings, not machines. Even machines are oiled and over-hauled. I don't think the people in charge there have got it right.'

Feng thought: He's making it all up.

'Their management needs looking into. Why should we copy it blindly? Don't communists believe in dialectics? Issuing orders isn't the best way to run an industry – material incentives often work better.'

Feng's hackles were up. As Ho paused for breath he put in, 'Daqing's a red banner set up by Chairman Mao, don't forget that!'

'I'm not saying everything about Daqing is wrong. During the three hard years from 1959 when we had no oil the Daqing oil field saved us from destitution. Everyone at Daqing made an immense contribution. During the Cultural Revolution, when the Gang of Four nearly bank-rupted the country, Daqing kept up production. But every-thing changes. Even the best have room for improvement. Why not try to do better than Daqing? Is that hacking down a red banner, turning revisionist? Just wait and see. Some day Daqing will be outclassed, because life moves forward, grows richer. . .'

Feng gave no sign of his bewilderment at Ho's outpourings. Stifling a yawn he decided that the crux of this harangue was Ho's opposition to Daqing, the red banner. So how to cope with him? Expressing a personal opinion of anybody or anything was risky. The political situation changed so quickly. A man you slammed today might be riding high tomorrow. It was always better to leave yourself a way out.

All Feng said was, 'If you won't write your plan for learning from Daqing, your section may not be made a Daqing-style section, and that could affect our whole bureau! Will you accept the responsibility if we fail to become a Daqing-style bureau?'

'That'll be nothing to do with me. Can't I work properly without learning from Daqing? Where have all these years of learning from Daqing got us? The time could have been much better spent. For instance by ending the friction in our section and the problems of our cadres.'

Ho could have expatiated upon what was wrong with the bureau's political work. But he knew it would be useless.

Feng refused to argue. If he did Ho might bring up even more embarrassing problems. Since the Cultural Revolution it seemed no subject was taboo, not even Central Committee directives or the private lives of leaders. It was hard nowadays being a leader. Nobody would have dared talk to him like this in the old days.

Yes, everyone looked back nostalgically to the fifties. If Ho had talked like this in 1957, he would have been labelled a Rightist. No wonder his application to join the Party had been turned down. He would have been a menace in the Party.

Better send him away and let Grace cope with him.

That evening, when leaving the office, Ho saw Wan Qun – Joy – standing in the slush frowning. She called to him, 'Ho, it's Sunday tomorrow. Will you help me fetch coal briquettes?'

'Why not let the factory deliver them?'

'They've stopped delivering, and I'm nearly out of coal. I'll have to get some myself.'

She'd had a hard time bringing up a child on her own. Why didn't she remarry? Well, he couldn't advise her on marriage again. If he hadn't put his oar in before, her life might not have been so tragic.

In 1962 when Joy left college and was assigned to their ministry, she had been an outstandingly attractive girl. If you told her about someone with four ears she'd tip her head to one side, open her eyes wide and exclaim credulously, 'Really?' The most nonsensical jokes reduced her to fits of laughter.

Everybody teased her. She had been so naive, so trusting. But she had lost her naiveté. Her eyes were sunken, the corners of her lips which had once curved up mischievously now seemed weighed down by worry. She was so thin that the veins on her forehead stood out. She was a widow and she looked it too. Her husband had committed suicide under political pressure in 1970.

Ho Jiabin should never have urged them to marry. But who could have foreseen what would happen? Marriage was a lottery. She and her husband had known each other at college. Though he studied engineering he enjoyed art, music and literature. And he was so handsome, he seemed cut out for Joy.

'You ought to marry Joy before someone else gets there,' Ho had advised him.

'Why don't you court her yourself?'

'Impossible! I can only appreciate women as works of art: I don't want to spoil their beauty. If I saw my wife pregnant or suckling a baby, I'd feel I'd committed a crime. That would kill my love for her.'

'What an aesthete you are, you nonsensical eccentric! And why do you tell *me* to marry her?'

Did Ho the aesthete know that only after marriage can a man and woman understand each other?

Joy had not had a happy marriage. And now that she was a widow life was even harder for her. But she was a strong-willed woman, reluctant to be indebted to anyone.

A car was honking – they were in its way. Ho drew Joy aside.

Through the window of the car they saw Fang's cold inscrutable face.

Ho told Joy, 'Right, I'll go with you at nine tomorrow morning.' To his surprise, tears glinted in her eyes.

What was wrong? How neurotic she'd grown!

4

This block of flats must have dated from the early fifties, when rooms had higher ceilings. It seemed a long climb up to the third floor. Though Autumn's health was not bad, her lined face and heart trouble showed that at forty-five she was ageing fast, gradually wearing out. Still, age had not made her any uglier, and her heart kept pumping away. . .

By the second floor she was winded. She leaned against the banisters to rest, wondering what reception she would get from the top official she was going to interview.

The staircase resounded with the chopping of fillings for dumplings, crying babies, a piano. . . Sundays were always lively. The piano piece was the simple 'Maiden's Prayer'. But the pianist was having trouble with it. Autumn had often played this song on the old untuned piano in one corner of her school assembly hall, as the sun slanted through the tall poplars and big windows on to the floor. In those days she had dreamed girlish dreams. In university she had seldom played the piano and had had no time to dream. . . But after starting work she had saved up to buy one. Through the ten years of the Cultural Revolution that piano had been silent, covered by an old rug. Now that it was possible to play again she was seldom in the mood. The dreams of girlhood belonged to another world.

The familiar melody so badly played brought bitter-sweet tears to her eyes.

As if to oppose the pianist someone was hammering away loudly.

Autumn was rather surprised that a vice-minister in the Ministry of Heavy Industry should be living in such second-rate housing. These were not flats for just anybody of course, but for middle-ranking officials. Not the sort of place, though, where most ministers lived. Because of this, she had a favourable impression of Vice-minister Zheng before she'd even met him.

His flat was the one where one person was playing the piano and someone else was hammering.

She had to knock hard before the pianist stopped playing.

The door opened. The girl who opened it had soft, brown, naturally curly hair cut very short, not much longer that Mo Zheng's. She was slightly cross-eyed but, oddly enough, instead of detracting from her prettiness this only made her more striking. Her white polo-neck sweater clung to her slender figure. Autumn had hardly ever seen anyone so graceful. But her trousers were baggy enough to hide a stolen chicken in and badly crumpled too.

As usual, when anyone met her for the first time, Autumn saw that the girl was thinking: 'Heavens, what an ugly woman!' But there was sympathy in this kind-hearted girl's eyes. It was evidently she who had been playing the piano, and Autumn at once forgave her inept performance.

'Who have you come to see?' A soft, sweet voice.

'Is Minister Zheng at home?'

'Who are you?'

Autumn produced her journalist's card and letter of introduction. The girl showed an interest in the journalist's card. She invited Autumn in, then went into another room. The hammering stopped.

The flat was very clean but did not look lived in. There were no pictures or photographs on the walls. All the furniture was ministry issue, and no attempt had been made at a colour scheme. Even the pale blue curtains were the kind seen in offices. Such a flat gave no indication of its occupants' tastes or hobbies. Autumn marvelled to see reflected here her own careless way of life.

'You want to see me?'

She turned. To her surprise Zheng was dressed very casually. He might have been a graduate of Oxford or Cambridge. Impossible, from what Ho had told her. He was very thin but had a powerful handshake.

'Why didn't you go through the ministry?' he asked brusquely. 'Do sit down.'

30

'The ministry promised to fix an appointment. But you always seemed to be busy, and I'm in a bit of a hurry myself.'

'Oh!' Zheng sized her up. This woman seemed as hard as a man. Yuanyuan had told him that she was a reporter.

Only then did Autumn notice that his eyes were too large for his lean face. As a small boy, she thought, he must have been most attractive.

This was a weakness of hers, letting her thoughts wander.

'I wanted to interview you,' she explained.

At once Zheng looked forbidding, as if averse to being written up or praised. 'I'm sorry, but there's nothing I can tell you.'

Was he averse to being written up or praised? Or perhaps he took this attitude because in the last ten years reportage had lost all credibility?

'No, I don't want to write you up. I want to ask your views on how industry should be modernized.'

He showed interest. 'Did your paper give you this assignment?'

'No, it's my own idea.' She repeated Mo Zheng's scathing comments on what was wrong with things.

'Why the great interest?'

'Because it affects a billion people's lives. Without the material base, we'll never be able to develop science, culture or defence. I wish I could make everyone take it seriously. My impression is that our investment programme is a shambles, but I don't know why it is, or how it can be set right. You know how much ordinary people expect from the economic policy-makers. Their lives are much harder than they need to be. Are we really so poor? I don't believe it. We wouldn't be, if we used our money properly like the Japanese. We pour it down the drain. I'll give you a trivial example. The road I take to work every day has been torn up three times in the last year. First for bigger sewage pipes; then for gas pipes; then for water mains. Or take the trees beside the road. The locust trees were cut down to plant poplars, then within two years they were replaced by

31

pines . . . Can't we make a long-term plan and stick to it? All this chopping and changing wastes so much labour and resources. Everyone knows it's wrong, so why do we keep doing it?'

This woman who looked so inflexible was actually as ingenuous as a child. Zheng asked her, 'Remember the first sentence in the *Communist Manifesto?*'

'"A spectre is haunting Europe – the spectre of Communism. All the Powers of old Europe have entered into a holy alliance to exorcise this spectre: Pope and Czar, Metternich and Guizot, French Radicals and German police-spies."'

'Splendid. And the last sentence, remember that?'

'"Working Men of All Countries, Unite!"' It was like a child's recitation in the classroom. What was he thinking? That it was just a stream of consciousness?

Zheng stood up, his hands behind his back, and paced swiftly to and fro. After a few minutes he asked, 'What brought you to *me?*'

'A man I was at university with works in your ministry. He told me you were a vice-minister with an open mind, guts and drive.' Autumn winced as she said it: it sounded like deliberate flattery.

Sure enough, Zheng knitted his brows.

'What's he called? Which section does he work in?'

'He's Ho Jiabin, in . . .'

'Yes, I know him. But it's ages since he came to see me.'

'He's a bit of an eccentric.'

'He's pathologically proud, like a lot of intellectuals. But he's a very good man.'

Autumn smiled. 'How do you know?'

'Why do you ask?'

'Your view doesn't seem to be shared by your director in charge of political work.'

Zheng smiled sarcastically.

'At university we worked on a magazine together,' she went on. 'Argued ourselves red in the face over a name for it. He wanted to call it "The X-Ray Lab", but the others voted him down because it might be taken for a medical journal. He got really worked up. Said a paper should diagnose society's diseases. It sounds ridiculous now. Rather touching too. It's not everyone who retains that naive capacity for caring about things, doesn't let life corrupt him. That's what I like about Ho. After twenty punishing years his face may be lined, but he hasn't changed at heart. Working for a newspaper I know that his views are impractical. But we shouldn't be afraid to tell the truth. We say our press must represent the Party. Does that really mean making out that everything's fine? That's cost us a terrible price. I'm no politician, not even a good reporter. I may think like this, but in fact I'm just a cog in the machine. Do you know the basic weakness of our generation? We don't understand our times.'

Zheng stopped pacing while she drank some tea. He noticed that she liked Longjing tea too. Yet she was not at all like his wife. She seemed always to be thinking, always questioning. What if a billion minds were to work like hers?

How could he explain to her all the obstacles in the way of reforming industry? It was all so complicated. Should he give her some data and research papers to look at? Yes, he would get his secretary to send her some.

'Excuse me, could you tell me your name?'

'Ye Zhiqiu,' Autumn replied.

'That's a beautiful name.' It suited her.

'Yes, it's wasted on someone like me.'

'No,' he found himself saying. 'Bitter gourds are bitter, but some people like them very much.' Then he realized he had said too much.

Why was she so sensitive? Maybe she was a bit neurotic. Apart from his wife, Zheng had no dealings with women outside the ministry, so did not know how to get on with them. As she was so different from his wife he couldn't humour her or throw dust in her eyes. She was too level-headed for flattery.

'I like the comparison,' she said, and he was sure she meant it.

Time slipped away.

They discussed economics, philosophy, politics . . . A professional woman, her mannerisms as they talked were like those of a man. When worked up she would pace to and fro, her hands behind her back, despite the fact that she had never before visited a vice-minister. Sometimes both paced in opposite directions, sometimes they stood in the middle of the room to talk.

Strange, his wife was an old Party member like himself. But it was years since they had discussed subjects like these. Was he to blame? Most of his waking hours were spent at the office or attending meetings. He seldom had a free Sunday and they slept in different rooms. Even at home he was preoccupied with business and too tired by then to chat. When he did, Bamboo never listened seriously or showed any genuine interest.

Had she withered mentally as well as physically? The loveliest women must age, grow wrinkled. Why did so many of them devote their energy to keeping tabs on their husbands instead of cultivating their own minds?

Love is not the monopoly of young men and girls. Old couples should try not to let their marriages stale. They had to be tended carefully like plants. A marriage wasn't a broom to be brought home and tossed behind the kitchen door. Women who failed to understand this were fools.

For all her fashionable clothes and good grooming, Bamboo never laughed heartily for fear of wrinkling her skin. Although nearly sixty she looked in her late forties, her complexion fair and unblemished. You had to look hard to detect the faint crow's-feet round her eyes. Yet Zheng felt that since their marriage Bamboo had been like a lady going home from a fancy-dress ball, who at once dropped her charming smile and grace of movement to wash off her make-up, take off her artificial eyelashes, padded bra and corsets, and shuffle about in a dressing-gown and old slippers, glaring for no reason at all and scolding the whole household. . . Did all women change like this?

Bamboo's expectations had been high at marriage. When they were disappointed she had started sulking.

Dusk was falling, making everything in the room indistinct. Autumn felt completely at home here, as if she had turned somersaults and listened to her grandmother's stories on this narrow sofa as a girl. She had just realized it was time to leave when the mistress of the household came back.

Bamboo tossed her handbag on the sofa without noticing the visitor and called, 'Yuanyuan!'

In general she paid no attention to other people: it was up to them to notice her. If any guests deserving attention came, she knew from their Toyotas or Mercedes-Benzes parked outside.

Zheng made the introduction with a frown: 'This is Comrade Ye Zhiqiu, a reporter.'

Bamboo slowly turned and nodded. 'Do sit down.' Before Autumn could answer she called 'Yuanyuan!' again.

Bamboo always closed her eyes after glancing around, and the undue deliberation of all her movements seemed very arrogant.

Yuanyuan came in, her tousled hair showing that she had been lying down.

'Reading in bed again! I've told you often enough it'll ruin your eyesight. Women who wear glasses are frumps.' She had forgotten or not noticed that their visitor wore glasses.

Yuanyuan and Zheng froze with embarrassment. But Autumn remarked casually, 'Yes, reading in bed is bad for the eyes.'

Bamboo opened a large paper parcel. 'I've bought you a sky blue goosedown anorak. It's warm and light. All the girls wear them nowadays.'

Zheng paid no attention but said, 'Let's have supper now.' He turned to Yuanyuan. 'Ask Mrs Wu to serve the meal.'

Shrewd Mrs Wu, the servant, came out of the kitchen in her apron to ask, 'Comrade Xia, shall I dish up now?'

Bamboo glanced at her watch. 'All right.' She added, 'We have a guest, so can you cook something extra?'

Autumn noticed that the gold watch-chain on her smooth white wrist looked tight – she was putting on weight.

Mrs Wu wiped her hands on her apron. 'As it's Sunday I bought plenty, I thought there might be guests. Got a chicken on the free market for over seven yuan. . . '

'Over seven yuan!' exclaimed Bamboo.

'It was a live one. And several pounds of yellow croakers too. . . '

Autumn noticed Zheng's sarcastic smile. When their eyes met, his glance seemed cold. She promptly took her leave.

'Won't you stay for supper?' he asked. 'We're having a chicken that cost over seven yuan!'

She suddenly sympathized with him. This highly re-spected vice-minister, in charge of tens of thousands of enterprises and over a million workers, had his headaches like everyone else. Life mocked him too.

Zheng could not make her out. Had they really just had that interesting discussion?

A visitor came in calling, 'I'm here to cadge a meal. Anything good to eat?'

'Come in, Minister Wang. It's good to see you.' Even the arrival of a guest like this only made Bamboo slightly more animated.

Wang Fangliang stared at Autumn. 'Haven't we met?'

'She's a reporter,' Zheng explained.

'Oh, a reporter! We have to butter up reporters, Zheng, or they'll write damning articles about us.' Wang spoke with a booming voice, as if addressing a hall full of people. 'Have you been interviewing him?' he asked. 'If so, you've picked the wrong man. He's a heretic. To be brutally frank, you can't be very hard-headed if you've decided to interview someone like him. Been expounding your theories on modernization, Zheng?'

Bamboo shot Autumn a glance both envious and disap-proving.

As Yuanyuan saw Autumn downstairs she asked, 'Where do you live? I'd like to come and see you.'

Autumn knew she was trying to made amends for her mother's rudeness.

A woman like that should have been able to keep her husband's love. But theirs didn't seem a happy family.

Vice-minister Wang Fangliang lolled back on a sofa, his legs crossed, his socks coming down. He kicked off his shoes, pulled off his socks and shook them. 'Such shoddy goods,' he growled.

For once Bamboo frowned. But only for a moment. She didn't want a lined forehead. 'You're right. I bought a washing-machine, and it broke down after we'd only used it a few times.'

'Just goes to show!' boomed Wang. 'If even Bamboo's worried about the quality of our products, the problem must be serious.'

'It's the same with our machines.' Zheng seemed to be gloating.

'Yes,' Wang sighed. 'Take a simple case. Our generators leak, but can we set that right? No!'

Bamboo fidgeted. This was much less interesting than socks or washing-machines. She smoothed her uncreased jacket and crossed her legs.

Wang could tell what she was thinking. He knew that even if no photographers were present she always posed in company. To be in the same room with her was tiring.

He couldn't fathom how Zheng had put up with her all these years. And yet he felt rather sorry for Bamboo. All women had their foibles: maybe that was their attraction.

'How've you been lately?' he asked.

'Not too bad,' she answered.

Ignoring her, Zheng said, 'A lot of quality problems could be avoided if we just stuck to the rules. We've tried persuasion and we've tried bonuses. Nothing wrong with either − but why don't they work? All these years we've relied on hot air and slogans, or pinning labels on people.

In theory the workers are the masters of the country. But how much have we done to ease their sufferings and their poverty? Do we encourage their initiative? What rights do they have? I know that the country's poor and we can't solve these problems overnight, but how much do we really care? Just think how close our political cadres were to the masses in the war years. Not any more. What we've got to do now is to bring back some of that lost hope and enthusiasm. This is a science, and we ought to study it.

'You mean the behaviourism that Professor Dai talked about?'

'I'd call it industrial psychology.'

Bamboo always listed tolerantly when Zheng held forth, like a sober and reasonable wife whose husband talks nonsense when drunk.

He could say anything he pleased, so long as it didn't lose him his mandarin's hat. So she sat there looking enthralled to demonstrate that she was no ignorant housewife, and to show respect for their distinguished guest, while taking in not a single word.

'Zheng's been meaning to call on that professor to find out about those theories of his,' she said. She had no idea what behaviourism was, but as science was all the rage now she tried to sound scientific.

'Well, this is something that interests both Wang and me but we don't expect to become instant Buddhas. The problems must be investigated and solved.'

Zheng's matter-of-fact comment sounded to Bamboo like a reprimand. She stood up. 'Let's have supper. We can talk afterwards.'

There weren't too many dishes, but they were well cooked.

Bamboo took her time over the meal, her small, even teeth patiently stripping each chicken-bone.

Zheng ate, as he did everything, in moderation.

Yuanyuan stuffed food into her mouth as if this were some chore to hurry though. Her mother looked disapprovingly at the rice and vegetables dropped round her bowl.

Wang fell to heartily, making himself at home. He urged Zheng, 'Have some more soup.'

'I've had enough.'

'Put down that beer and have some soup instead. You've got to have a main target whether you're eating, fighting or working.'

Yuanyuan giggled. 'Uncle Wang, I think everything is your main target!'

'Yuanyuan, you mustn't say such things to grown-ups,' Bamboo reproved her.

'Why not?' said Wang. 'I got up rather late for my trip to Red East Commune this morning, and kept tripping over things in my hurry. I asked my boy, "Why don't you put your things away properly?" He had an answer to that: "I just tripped over the shoes you left in the middle of the study. You set a bad example." He was right. We have to let young people have their say.'

'How was it, your visit to the commune?' asked Zheng.

'Tian Shoucheng put me on the spot.' He paused to whet Zheng's curiosity.

The commune had written to Minister Tian complaining that the tractor they had bought was so badly made it was useless – a complete waste of money. The factories under their ministry received endless complaints of this kind; but in his reports to the State Council, Tian always managed to find some excuse.

This time, for once, he had reacted strongly, sending Wang and the factory manager to fetch back the defective tractor, apologize to the commune and promise to replace it with a good one.

Perhaps it was because a new wind was blowing, heralding reforms. Not only in the economic system but every other field. But Tian has misjudged the weather before, notably in the middle of 1976. A high official who has lost his principled Party stand is liable to become an opportunist.

Tian wondered: Would he benefit from these reforms? Or lose out?

No other ministry had yet taken back defective equipment. Judging by the present climate of opinion this was likely to be publicized in the mass media. So it seemed a good bet.

At the Party branch meeting Zheng had guessed that Wang was set on going to the Red East Commune for some ulterior motive.

'Yesterday I told my secretary to ring up the county committee to invite all the commune cadres and nearby commune members to attend. Today I discovered that the hall would hold only a few hundred people. So I said, "Let's have our meeting in the square." When the county secretary objected that it would be cold I told him, "Never mind, we're Party members. The more people hear our self-criticism the better." So a few tables were put together in the square and they fixed up a loud-speaker. Then I announced, "Comrade commune members, I'm here as a vice-minister to apologize for selling you a substandard tractor. We fell down on our job and virtually cheated you out of all that hard-earned money. That factory produces the worst tractors in the whole country. Don't buy any more of them. If you've bought them, send them back!" Of course the factory manager was livid. He thought it served me right to have spent years in jail during the Cultural Revolution, and wished I were still there. But as I outrank him he didn't dare protest. Hauling tractors back shouldn't be the end of it either. He can't be allowed to go on producing defective ones. Why do managers like him have life tenure, no matter if they lose money or how incompetent they are?

'The people shouted, "We need tractors, where can we get them?"

'I said, "Apply to the Liming Tractor Works. Their tractors are good and cheap." We need competition. I told them you'd got Liming to advertise in the paper instead of factories having exclusive selling rights. If a factory produced goods that wouldn't sell so that the wages couldn't be paid, the workers would raise hell and managers would have to find some way out.

'One Party secretary asked me, "Is it right to let the means of production circulate freely? Marx never said so."

'I told him, "There's a lot Marx never said. Can't we use our own heads? Marx would have been in favour of anything that helped our socialist economy to develop and speeded up modernization."'

This said, Wang roared with laughter, looking extremely smug.

'Uncle Wang, I think you're great! Just what a minister should be. If all ministers were like Uncle Tian, I could be a minister too. He never commits himself to anything.'

'Yuanyuan!' Zheng frowned.

Yuanyuan rolled her eyes and pouted. 'But it's true!'

Wang teased, 'How can you say such things about your future father-in-law?'

'I wouldn't have *him* for a father-in-law!'

'It's no secret that you're going steady with his son.'

Bamboo looked put out: Wang really had no tact.

'Him? He's the last person I'd have as a friend.'

'How can you talk like that? What's wrong with him?' Bamboo scolded.

Yuanyuan kicked back her chair spilling soup all over the table, and flounced out of the room.

'Why bring up that business of advertising in the paper?' Zheng asked, ignoring this fracas.

'I admire your guts, Zheng!' As old colleagues they knew each other well, yet Wang had been most impressed by Zheng's assuming responsibility for the Liming advertisement. That summer they had only just started to talk about the market, profit, competition. . . If the policy were suddenly reversed, then Zheng would be in trouble. Admiring Zheng's disregard for his own interests, he fished out a packet of cigarettes and offered him one.

Zheng waved it aside.

Wang's eyes flashed with mockery. 'Against your wife's orders?'

'I smoked too much this afternoon.'

From another pocket Wang fished out a small box of

chewing-gum. 'Guaranteed to make you stop smoking. Want to try one?'

Zheng said nothing.

Wang chuckled, 'A wife's orders have to be obeyed. But I can't give up smoking completely. So I smoke and chew this gum to please both parties.'

Trust Wang Fangliang to steer a middle course. But would he be able to go on like that?

In the past everyone had talked only of class struggle, of fights to the death. As if violent clashes could only occur between enemy camps. Surely it should be easier to solve conflicting views in the same camp? There was no vocabulary to describe the present sharp confrontation. What they were up against now were deeply ingrained beliefs. These beliefs were like a net in which all were caught. History was bound to condemn and eliminate them. Yet the people frantically defending these beliefs were their good comrades.

Communists should impel society forward.

Today's heresies would soon be seen as right and proper.

5

The small alarm-clock by the bed showed 6.10 a.m., time to get up. She could hear traffic outside. The wife of the manager of a motor works, she was specially sensitive to the noise of engines. She could recognize heavy trucks, tip-up lorries, jeeps and cars by the sound they made.

She meant to cook Chen Yongming a really good lunch; he so seldom had a day off. Food tasted different when shared with him. Their flat seemed warmer too when he was home. She smiled at herself: silly to be so obsessed with her husband.

But Yu Liwen – Radiance – went on lying in bed, not wanting to disturb her husband. She turned her head quietly to scan his lean face on the pillow.

Worn out, fast asleep, he still looked worried. His eyes were sunken. Although not yet sixty his hair was turning white, and it needed cutting. He hadn't shaved either. When she had pressed her face to his last night, the stubble on his chin had pricked her.

'How long since you last shaved?' she had asked.

He had simply smiled, his thoughts wandering.

She had tapped him on the forehead. 'What are you thinking about?'

'Nothing special. I feel there's something I've forgotten.' To make up for his coldness he had kissed her. But still she had felt his mind was on something else.

Chen had married late. He would probably have missed out on love and marriage if he hadn't been hospitalized with acute hepatitis in 1962. He had been thirty-seven then, and she twenty-three, an intern fresh from medical college.

Every day he lay staring at the door of his ward to watch the white-coated intern flash past or come up to his bed with a smile.

He discovered the existence of something else besides production and the state plan that could absorb his spirit and energy.

His courtship was like his work. He took her by storm.

Some people thought them ill-matched; he was warned that she was not a Party member.

Her sweet eyes anxious, she asked, 'Am I good enough for you? Can I make you happy?'

He held her close. 'You were born for me, little girl!'

What an odd romance it had been.

As soon as she came off duty, she would miss her supper to nestle in his arms. 'What, haven't you eaten? I'm to blame. Hit me!' He raised her small hand to slap him. Then they would spend half the short time he could spare her looking for somewhere to eat.

Sometimes she waited for a couple of hours on a bench in the park, till he hurried indignantly towards her. 'Let's get married,' he'd urge. 'We can't go on like this. I haven't the time.'

Or he might phone, 'Sorry, I can't get away. I love you . . . Why don't you say anything?' He might raise his voice.

'All right, I may have half an hour free at ten. Can you come to my office?'

So one summer afternoon he had led her by the hand to the registry office.

The scorching sun and her wild emotions made her dizzy.

They stood under a locust tree. A caterpillar fell on her neck, making her cry out softly. She rested her head on his broad shoulder, her eyes moist. He took out a big crumpled handkerchief to wipe her perspiring forehead. 'What is it? What's wrong?'

Radiance had never known him sound so frantic. It wasn't in character. No catastrophe could make him panic. To him she meant more than anyone in the world, but he saw no need to put this into words.

Their newly furnished bridal chamber seemed strangely bare.

Chen bustled about at random, moving boxes from place to place.

Finally he flung up his hands and told her, 'Sorry, I ought to have a wash.'

'Shall I boil some water for you?' She wasn't accustomed yet to this new home, hadn't found her right place in it.

'No need, thanks.' He washed himself under the cold tap in the lavatory.

His face shone below his wet hair still smelling of soap.

'Shall we get supper, little wife?' But they couldn't find a cooking-pan among all the new furniture.

So on their wedding night they dined on biscuits . . .

After that their life was happy.

They had too little time together. One kiss from her husband transported Radiance for days. But she often had to wait a long time for his next caress. He had so many business trips. Still, as they say, absence makes the heart grow fonder.

She was proud of being Chen Yongming's wife, though it was hard. Hadn't she dreamed as a girl of having a strong husband she could look up to?

The Cultural Revolution brought her fearful anxiety and distress: he was nearly beaten to death. When he came back after several months' confinement in a damp room he could hardly walk for arthritis. His broad back was bent and he limped along leaning against the wall. Her heart bled for him. She searched everywhere for good medicine, made hot compresses for his joints, until he teased, 'All men should marry doctors.'

She smiled, but couldn't hold back her tears. When he pulled her close she turned her head away, unwilling to meet his eyes.

'Aren't I doing fine?' he demanded. 'Once I'm well again I'll carry you on my back up the Western Hills . . .'

He recovered. But his hair was turning grey, and in wet weather his joints ached and creaked. He could not hide this from a doctor's eyes.

Of course they had no time to go the Western Hills.

Two years before, Vice-minister Zheng Ziyun had come to tell Chen they wanted to appoint him manager of the Dawn Motor Works.

'Our Party branch thinks you're just the man for the job.'

'I've never run so big a plant.'

'It's riddled with problems. There's been a rapid turn-over of managers. Of course, in the days of the Gang of Four nothing could be done. Now the time's ripe to modernize, but there are endless obstacles. There's a big disagreement on how the economy should be developed. If only the people who make the decisions were clear-headed and determined. Why do some people still doubt whether the aim of production is to raise living standards? Some old Party members have never really grasped Marxism, although they may be good comrades . . . That's how it is . . . I'll give you a few days to think it over.'

Not only did Chen think it over, so did his friends. Those who knew the works told him he'd never make a go of things there.

Chen wondered if he was up to it. Did he have enough drive and ability?

Ten days later Chen asked Zheng, 'What exactly do you want me to do?'

'The first two things are simple. Output must go up each month till it's double last year's figures. And production must be balanced. That plant is such a shambles, it won't be easy. You'll have your work cut out. Any conditions?'

'It's a tough job, and I hope to succeed. But I'll need full authority. Will you give me that?'

'The ministry will certainly delegate all the authority it can to you.' Zheng reflected for a moment, and added, 'Within limits.'

'Suppose I clash with the existing management?'

'So long as you abide by objective economic laws, I'll back you up to the hilt. Take all the responsibility I can. If anyone lodges complaints I'll help you get by.'

Chen seldom put into words his gratitude or admiration. Now, impulsively, he reached out to clasp Zheng's hand.

Each time Chen talked with Zheng, he felt stimulated and strengthened. Not all those in leading posts had Zheng's ability to size up their subordinates. He had drive too, could set goals and give the men under him confidence to reach them. Cadres were glad to work under him, regardless of the difficulties involved.

Radiance was sure that whatever decisions her husband reached were right. At forty she still took a simplified, girlish view of our complex society. In some ways this was all to the good. She was no politician for ever analyzing the dangers, increasing her husband's worries or advising him on policy decisions. Instead, with wifely concern she used her medical knowledge to take care of his health and give him moral support.

As she stroked Chen's hair someone tapped at the door. She heard suppressed laughter, an argument in low voices.

Their sons. The twins. He had promised to take them skating today. In their excitement the boys had got up without being called. They rarely had a chance to go out with their father.

Radiance decided to ignore them and let her husband lie in. They boys must have guessed this, for they scampered off.

But Chen woke up, his face animated again. He took his wife's hand, kissed her ten fingers in turn, then loudly cleared his throat. The central heating was so hot that each morning he woke up parched.

The next moment the door was flung open and the twins shot in. Their father got up and they clung to his outstretched arms, the three of them whirling round and round like a windmill.

In the queue for yellow croakers, she saw the wives of the former heads of the Daqing Office and the Political Section chattering excitedly. They beckoned her over. 'Fresh croakers today. Come and stand with us.'

'No, I can't jump the queue. Besides, I'm not buying fish.' Radiance flushed with embarrassment and slipped away.

'A hypocrite – just like her husband!' was one woman's comment.

'Yet the way they carry on! Did you hear about when Chen Yongming came back from Japan? They clung to each other at the airport in front of everyone.' The other sniggered. 'Couldn't they wait to get home?'

'Intellectuals!'

'Yes, intellectuals are doing nicely now. They've had their tails in the air ever since Deng Xiaoping* said that they're workers too.' The speaker ground her teeth.

---

* A veteran revolutionary, twice disgraced in earlier years, Deng Xiaoping returned to power in 1978 and is generally considered responsible for the sweeping changes which took place after the death of Mao Zedong.

47

This was how these two wives vented their indignation. Before Chen's appointment their husbands had been respected and feared; then, overnight, they had lost their cushy jobs.

6

Li Ruilin arrived early for the morning shift. He stood by the factory gate with very mixed feelings. During his two months' absence without leave from work his mind had been in a turmoil. It was strange that a Party secretary who for years had cracked down on others for being discontented was now so disgruntled himself.

At first he had been angry. What did the new manager Chen Yongming mean by removing the full-time Party secretaries of each workshop. Since taking over he had been doing unheard-of things. Hadn't he been bashed hard enough in the Cultural Revolution?

But after being ignored for two months Li Ruilin decided to go to see Chen himself.

Chen asked him bluntly, 'Got used to the idea yet?'

'Never mind about that. Give me something to do first.'

'That's the spirit.' But Chen went on, 'I've told the accounts office to pay you for one week's leave on private business, not for the rest of the time. As Party members we should stick to our posts, even if we don't like what's happening. You ought to know that after all those years of political work.' Chen's expression had hardened and he looked irritated.

Chen knew quite well that docking his pay would enrage not only Li but other malcontents too, who might make an issue of it. Especially now that prices were going up. Already they were out for his blood. But each step forward, each decision he took, even on some piddling question like buying mugs, seemed to him a small link in the chain of a great struggle.

It was difficult. Was he rushing things? He had been careful to compromise on certain issues. Last time Minister Tian turned up, Chen had agreed to reimburse the costs of his entertainment, but had added, 'Only buy three packets of cigarettes. If they aren't smoked, don't open them but keep them for next time.' There had been comments about his stinginess, and although a whole carton had been bought he had stuck to his decision and not paid for the rest. Of course it made him unpopular; but as long as he had this post he meant to run the works in a business-like way.

After that no one dared to squander public funds. This aroused opposition but he got support as well.

What worried Chen was that Party members like Li resisted any measures affecting themselves. And he was bound to incur even more unpopularity in the course of streamlining production. All kinds of obstacles were put in his way. But when he lost heart, he made the rounds of the factory, noting problems to do with production or with the workers' welfare which needed to be solved. Then his depression melted away. He had to put all his energy into his work and organize his efforts more scientifically.

Though furious at having his pay docked, Li could not make a scene as he did not have a leg to stand on. But one thought – that he'd been over thirty years in the Party – rankled.

Old Lü greeted him just as before. 'You're early, Secretary Li.'

Li was tempted to say, 'Don't call me Secretary. Call me Old Li from now on.'

It was hard to take the idea that he'd belong with a janitor like Old Lü now. It was unheard of for a Party cadre to step down. In the old days only cadres who had committed serious mistakes were demoted some grades. The rest, if not promoted, should at least retain their posts. Whoever had heard of a Party secretary becoming a workman?

He took comfort from being addressed as 'Secretary'. At

49

any rate Old Lü didn't think that he was undergoing labour reform. So Li urged him to go home and rest.

Old Lü wheeled out his rusty bicycle and put on the army cap given him by his son Lü Zhimin when he was demobbed, and his patched, greasy padded coat. He should have bought a new coat long ago, but he was saving the money for his son.

Li had heard that Old Lü and his son kept quarrelling. Young Lü wasn't bad, but youngsters nowadays were a rough lot. They gave their parents no peace.

Li sat for a while in the janitor's room, then stood up, at a loose end. After all these years here he suddenly felt as awkward as a new hand.

He poked up the stove and put the kettle on, then fetched a broom to sweep the asphalt drive. Not that it needed sweeping. He straightened up to look round. He had come to this motor works over twenty years ago when he was demobbed. Had seen it start from scratch, then expand and become a show place. It was bigger now than the county town near his home. It took half an hour just to walk round it.

In front of the entrance was a large flower-bed round which ran two asphalt drives flanked by white poplars. Their branches had been pruned, leaving stumps like bulging eyes to keep a stern watch on all who came in, including Li Ruilin. Below was a hedge of soot-blackened dwarf pines.

The office building stood behind the garden. To its right was a huge parking lot where new trucks were neatly drawn up like recruits in new uniforms ready to be driven off. Even Li had to admit that producing these was no mean feat in a plant as disorganized as theirs, with so many people gunning for each other and passing the buck. He knew all the problems. Why wasn't Chen Yongming looking discouraged?

The kettle boiled. Li made himself a mug of jasmine tea. At eighty cents an ounce it was inferior to what had once cost sixty. He sat down to roll a cigarette, and slowly puffing it looked round the simply furnished room.

50

A neatly written list was pasted under the wall-clock.

A One Yuan Fine Will Be Imposed for the Following Offences:
1. Spitting on the floor
2. Smoking in the factory
3. Dropping litter
4. Parking outside the parking lot
5. Bringing in family members.
Dawn Motor Works.

This struck Li as a big fuss over nothing.

Weren't the roads outside strewn with litter, cigarette-stubs and gobs of spittle. Even in the main shopping streets you trod on vomit if you weren't careful. And you couldn't help spitting. All Chinese spat. You could hear hawking and spitting wherever you went. And what harm did it do anyway?

No doubt Chen Yongming had picked up these notions during his recent visit to Japan. Now the plant had built a green-house, taken on a gardener. This spring they were going to plant lawns. What use would those be? Could they make up for power cuts or shortages of material? A factory was a factory. If you wanted to see flowers you should go to a park. Why did they have to do things like foreigners?

Did he have it in for Chen?

Whose fault was it that he was now a janitor?

Since coming back from a meeting at the ministry this spring Chen had got even worse. There had been all that nonsense about industrial enterprises now having more initiative, about competing on the market. The management was to be reorganized; the Daqing Office and the Political Section were to be scrapped; and the workshops would no longer have full-time Party secretaries . . . And Chen really meant it.

Some things were more than Li could take.

Was it right to scrap the Political Section and the Daqing Office?

Chen had said, 'They're just forms. What counts is what we actually do. We must concentrate on solving the workers' problems and boosting production. We don't need a Political Section or a Daqing Office for that.'

The heads of different sections were to be appointed by the Party Committee after sounding out public opinion, and they would be allowed to appoint their own subordinates, like a prime minister appointing a cabinet. Wouldn't this lead to factionalism? How could a section head know better than the factory's Party Committee or Personnel Department? How could they run socialist industry in this bourgeois way?

Each time he had sat down for a meeting or for political study, Li would doze off to avoid joining in the discussion, for fear of exposing his ignorance of the new terms like 'cabinet'.

For when he had queried it, Yang Xiaodong, a firebrand in No. 2 Workshop, had retorted, 'That's no bourgeois expression. Didn't Chairman Mao warn Jiang Qing not to form her own cabinet?'*

Chen Yongming took a tough line. 'A section head can rope in anyone as long as he gets production up within three months. If he fails he'll have to step down. What's there to be afraid of? To get work done you need mates you get along with. It's no use preaching: "We're all Marxists, all class brothers, so everyone's bound to get on." Li Ruilin as secretary and Sheng Hongzhao as workshop head are both good comrades, yet how can they work together when they're at each other's throats all the time? Much better for them to split up. The Organization Department often put incompatible people in the same section. Or appointed men with seniority who simply weren't up to their jobs. That's part of the reason the plant's in such a mess. Now we're giving the sections and workshops more say; they'll elect more capable people. Our public opinion poll shows that we've got the talents but don't know how to use them.'

* It is rumoured that Mao Zedong issued this warning to Jiang Qing in the year before he died.

52

So Li Ruilin had lost his post as secretary, lost even his rank as a cadre. It was incredible: no one had accused him of any serious fault, but no one wanted him. Or take Feng, the head of No. 4 Workshop and a model worker.

Chen had said, 'Why need a model be made an official? We need managers who understand technology and can organize production. Feng will take on the hardest jobs and work overtime till he drops; but No. 4 Shop is a mess, and never meets its monthly targets. He can't give clear instructions or take notes. As a model worker he's fine, but a workshop is more than he can handle.'

'That's not his fault. He had no education. You can't expect us hicks to be scholars.' Li squared his shoulders.

'You could talk that way just after Liberation, because before that we'd been fighting a war. But we've had thirty years of peace. How've you spent them? Playing poker!'

'What's wrong with poker?' Li demanded. He thought: I don't drink or smoke, and playing cards isn't a vice. Why pick on minor faults, avoiding the main problem?

Someone nominated Miao Zhuoling to head No. 4 Shop.

Li objected, 'His family origin is bad and he has a doubtful record.'

Chen fumed, 'Still on about that sort of thing? Goodness knows how many good comrades have been destroyed that way. It's kept down so many talents, it's been a national disaster too. For years we've been marking time. In the fifties our economy was pretty well on a par with Japan's, but now we're at least thirty years behind.'

'They still have rats this size in their slums!' Li's hands indicated a rat as big as a cat.

'Have you ever seen one?'

'I've read it in the papers.'

There was a roar of laughter.

A bicycle bell broke into Li's reflections. Wu Guodong came riding in on a brand-new bike. He greeted Li, 'Back at work, eh?'

'Can't sit at home doing nothing,' Li snapped. He went out to have a good look at the bike, wondering how Wu had raised the money for it after being on sick leave for so long. It must have cost 170 yuan.

Wu explained, 'The plant is giving loans to people who have trouble getting to work because they live a long way away. We pay back two yuan a month from our pay.' He rang his bell with a smile of satisfaction. It was hard for a low-paid worker to buy a bike.

No one could accuse Chen Yongming of indifference to the workers. New housing was being built for them to solve a problem that had dragged on for years.

'Got over your hepatitis?'

'Yes.' Wu shook his head to convey the hard time he'd had.

'Well, take it easy, you don't want a relapse.'

Lü Zhimin cycled in, puffing at a cigarette. He made a token gesture of dismounting by touching the ground with the tip of one foot, and spat out the butt of his cigarette.

'You have to dismount at the gate!' bellowed Li.

'What's up?' Young Lü blinked.

'What's up? You're fined one yuan.'

'Why?'

'Read the notice.'

Young Lü rolled his eyes.

Both Li and Wu were gloating. They thought these fines ridiculous and hoped the workers would refuse to pay them.

At the meeting when Chen had scrapped the Daqing Office, Li had sprung up to protest, 'Are you refusing to take the socialist road?' The youngsters in the hall had hooted with laughter and whistled, Young Lü among them.

Old Wu put in, 'Manager Chen announced this to the whole staff, didn't he?'

Slowly Young Lü unbuttoned his jacket. He admired the new manager and would abide by his rules. But Wu's smug face annoyed him and he was trying to think of a retort. Never mind if Old Wu was his workshop head.

Li had a mental picture of Old Lü's ramshackle bicycle

and ragged coat. He suddenly changed his mind. 'All right. Remember next time. Pick up that cigarette butt and drop it in the dustbin.'

Young Lü did this, waved at Li, shot Wu a defiant glance and cycled off.

Wu was annoyed. These youngsters were the limit.

Yang Xiaodong had told Ge Xinfa and Wu Bin to meet him after lunch to discuss some business. They went to the canteen and found him there with Young Lü who, wearing outsize sun-glasses, had a sulky, listless expression on his face. Yang was grinning broadly and telling Lü off for his sun-glasses.

'Take them off! Are you an overseas Chinese?' Wu snatched off the sun-glasses.

'You elected me team leader,' Yang continued. 'So the thirteen of you should all behave like deputy leaders. Everyone's got to work out the best ways of doing their jobs. You agreed to that, didn't you?'

'Right,' said Lü.

He accepted whatever Yang said. In their team they all stood together. They were good mates.

Wu Guodong had once bawled him out for wearing flared trousers. Yang had spoken up for him: 'Bell-bottoms don't make you a hooligan.'

Lü's old man kept complaining about him to Yang too.

Last year, when Lü brought home a new wash-basin and two towels, his father had asked Yang if the lad had stolen them. He always ran his son down. Yang rebutted some of his accusations, and he talked the old man round on others. For this Lü respected him.

'OK,' he said. 'Next time I wear my glasses you can confiscate them.'

Wu returned the offending shades to Lü, then asked Yang, 'What did you want us for?'

Yang showed them the results of the opinion poll in the team on how to spend their fifty yuan bonus. All but one had opted for a meal in the nearby New Wind Restaurant.

'It's New Year's Eve,' Yang said. 'All we have to do this afternoon is tidy up. You and Ge needn't join in the cleaning up. You're the restaurant kings: you can order the meal and keep a table for us. At three o'clock we'll be through and we'll join you.'

Ge and Wu were gourmands. Whenever they got a bonus they blew it on food. Yang often urged them to save up to get married instead.

'Even if you have the money,' said Ge, 'you can't unless you have a room. Young Song practically went down on his knees to beg Wu Guodong for one.'

'I tell you what I would have done if I'd been in Song's shoes,' fumed Wu Bin. 'I'd have moved into his bloody office with my wife. He could have had us sleeping on his desk. Then what would he have done? He is a bastard.'

'No he isn't,' protested Yang. 'He's running the shop pretty well. He doesn't pull strings and he isn't looking after number one. When the factory bought a truckload of fruit and he heard it wasn't from a state shop, he refused to buy any. Old Wu isn't bad as cadres go. Besides, in a piddling little job like his there's not much he can do anyhow.'

'Well he's always got it in for us', Wu Bin insisted. 'When Young Song asked him for a room, he didn't even look up from the newspaper he was reading. Kept him standing there for ages, then asked, "Marry? How old are you?"

'"Twenty-seven. You asked me a couple of days ago."

'He'd forgotten. He ought to know what's on our minds, and see our good points too. The way you do, Xiaodong. Old Wu went on at him, "You must wait a few more years. There are people in their thirties in our shop who haven't been able to marry yet. Late marriage is state policy. As one of the working class your first duty is to the Party and the state." He really gets my goat. Treats us like dirt, and preaches at us all the time.'

Just after three, Wu Guodong noticed Yang's team take off their overalls, wash their hands and yell at each other to hurry. Only Wu Bin and Ge Xinfa were missing. He went to inspect Wu Bin's lathe – it was clean and freshly oiled.

The floor around it had been swept and the machined axle-covers were neatly stacked on a shelf. The tools had all been locked in their box. He could find nothing wrong. But he felt it his duty as Party secretary to ask Yang where they were all off to.

'To the New Wind Restaurant.'

'Who's paying?'

'We all are. Didn't you say the teams could spend their bonuses however they wanted.'

'We're going out for a spot of murder and arson,' said Young Lü, just to annoy him.

Wu watched them wheel out their bikes, each with its saddle raised to the maximum height, and pedal off like a swarm of locusts with a great ringing of bells.

In Wu Guodong's eyes they were indeed a swarm of locusts.

So they were throwing their bonus away on a blowout. The thought made his hair stand on end.

How the hell had all these awkward customers got into the turning-shop? They were as thick as thieves and did every-thing together. Even when pay rises were being discussed not one of them had come to him to complain about the others. In most teams there would be squabbles and angry recriminations over pay. Everyone needed money! What did he and his wife squabble over if not money?

If one of the team took a couple of days off sick the others would do his work for him so that he could still draw a bonus. Once Lü Zhimin had caught flu, but as he had no temperature the clinic had refused him sick leave. Yang Xiaodong had told him to rest and worked both their lathes.

Before 1978 the shop had never fulfilled its quota. The chassis team had blamed the turning-shop for holding them back and Wu had bawled them out time and again.

They had protested that it was not their fault, complaining that work was hopelessly chaotic. Since then the workshop had been reorganized and they had been a team of their own.

For two years now they had fulfilled their quota. This year they had been cited as an advanced team with its work always up to standard.

What was the reason? Political consciousness? No. There were only two Party members and three Youth League members among them.

Their team leader? Was Yang Xiaodong all that able? Wu knew that his father had belonged to the Kuomintang, and Yang was not a Party or Youth League member. In 1967 he had been reprimanded for driving a truck on the sly after the night shift. Nothing very bad, but the crafty way he'd covered it up showed he was a tricky character. What had given him such a hold over all his mates? Was it because they were a gang and saw Yang as their boss?

It could hardly be because they cared about their team's reputation, if they were willing to blow their bonus on a binge.

What motivated them? To Wu Guodong this was a riddle. So although their work was good he was keeping an eye on them.

But though he disliked Yang Xiaodong, he had to admit that this team leader did a good job.

The manager Chen Yongming obviously thought the world of these youngsters. He often talked to them about things like ecology, the trips made abroad by state leaders, the dangerous course taken by Khomeini . . . Sometimes they even used English or Japanese words. That was why they were hard to control – they knew too much.

Chen Yongming took their opinions seriously, especially Yang Xiaodong's views on workers' psychology. Chen urged all the workshop heads to master industrial psychology. He said it was because Yang grasped it so well that his team was so good.

Was psychology the secret? Old Wu was mystified.

7

The artist's heavy-jowled face was flaccid and wrinkled, yet there was childish wonder in his limpid eyes. Eyes which seemed out of keeping with his thought-provoking paintings. Looking at his eyes Zheng Ziyun felt a stab of envy. In his young days he had wanted to study anthropology, literature or history, but fate had made him an official.

The artist was a friend of Wang Fangliang's, who had friends of every description, from vice-premiers and antiquarians to cooks.

Zheng had praised a certain painting to Wang at an art exhibition.

Wang had laughed heartily. 'Good for you.' Then added seriously, 'This is a tricky time for artists.'

'Why?'

'We equate painting a nude with sleeping with her.' He roared with laughter again.

The painting was of several nude nymphs, lying outstretched. In a subtle way it conjured up the eternal secret of life. While the frailty of these figures aroused in men a sense of protectiveness, they also gave one a feeling of the power of dependency, the power that nurtures life and talent.

'Will you ask him if he's willing to sell it to me?'

The artist gave him the painting, making Zheng regret his impulsive request. Could he hang it up? What would his colleagues think? A man in his position had to be careful. But if he didn't hang it up he'd be letting the artist down.

He couldn't take it for nothing. Should he pay him? Wang said, 'Money means nothing to him. He might regard it as an insult.'

This had happened over a month ago, yet still it preyed on his mind.

So he suddenly decided to take the artist to a restaurant where they could have a good talk. He had been rather irritated all day, and was not in the mood to go home. A few days previously the State Economic Commission had asked the Ministry of Heavy Industry for a speech on its reorganization of the enterprises under its control. Tian Shoucheng had thrust this thankless job on to him, and told him to write a draft. It had been returned by the Commission this morning with the comment that they should stress that they had reorganized on the basis of learning from Daqing. Tian had agreed to this. When Zheng learnt about this from his secretary Ji he had torn up his draft with a bitter laugh.

'Ring up the Economic Commission. Tell them I'm not making the speech.'

Wang Fangliang had hastily stopped Ji and advised Zheng, 'It's enough that you sent in an outline of your speech. You can say what you like at the meeting. I think you'd better go.'

'No point!' Zheng was adamant.

'Well, that's up to you. Young Ji, tell them Vice-minister Zheng says our work isn't worth reporting.'

Ji Hengquan had been assigned to Zheng by the Personnel Department after Zheng got his old job back. He had not asked for a secretary. He drafted all his speeches himself, and felt no need to find patrons or followers to consolidate his position, which he was quite willing to lose.

Ji, who had worked for several ministers, was highly experienced. But he found Zheng Ziyun unpredictable and too temperamental. Ji suspected that he would never rise any higher. Or that, if he did, he would have a bad fall. He kept tabs on Zheng's correspondence, his telephone calls and his visitors. This might come in useful later.

Ji thought Zheng's reaction pathetically perverse. Zheng never considered the consequences of his actions. And he did not have the backing of any members of the Central Committee.

Ji decided to take Wang's advice. Wang Fangliang was more formidable though seemingly so jovial and easy-going. Even Minister Tian was rather afraid of him.

Bamboo was pestering Zheng on the telephone.

'Why won't you be home to supper?

'Who are you going out with?

'Who? Why've I never heard of him?' That painting had been hanging for at least a month in their sitting-room, where she saw it every day, but she never read the artist's name.

She scolded, 'Eating out on New Year's Eve! You might as well write your family off . . . Fangfang and Peiwen are coming for supper, but you're off to a restaurant with some artist or other.' She ground out the word 'artist' with contempt.

'At least I'm still free to choose where I eat,' drawled Zheng, ignoring her torrent of protests as he rang off.

Word of his son-in-law Peiwen's visit made him even more reluctant to go home. He disliked this upstart whom Bamboo had chosen for their elder daughter. The fellow's oily manner reminded him of small traders before Liberation.

Zheng felt sorry for his daughter Yuanyuan. He should have asked her out too, but he wasn't going to ring home again and hear his wife erupting like a volcano. Yuanyuan was his only tie with home. Although forty years apart in age, they spoke a common language.

The blind alley was too narrow even for a Toyota to turn in. Yang the driver had to back into it.

The small compound, probably once the home of a single family, had in it jujube trees, persimmon trees, jasmine and roses – real Beijing taste – but it was no longer quiet and peaceful now that it was shared by several households. Each had built its own kitchen in the courtyard, which reeked of cabbage, scallions, fried fish . . . Husbands and wives were quarrelling, children were howling, radios were turned on full blast . . .

The artist's studio was a small earthquake shelter put up in 1976.* It was cold now, but in summer must be scorch-

* After the great earthquake at Tangshan in the summer of 1976 earthquake shelters were put up all over Beijing.

ing. When you looked at the paintings on the wall, however, you forgot the poky room and the malodorous, noisy courtyard. China really gets its intellectuals on the cheap, Zheng thought. Then, remembering the technicians in his ministry and the workers in factories, he reflected that China got all its common people on the cheap.

In the car the artist blurted out, 'This is the first time since Liberation that a minister has ever . . .'

'A vice-minister,' Zheng corrected him.

'Not even a vice-director has ever been to our place. But it's not your rank that impresses me, it's your appreciation of art, your attitude to people.' He spoke fast, gripping the door handle, as if prepared to jump out should Zheng misunderstand.

Zheng was impressed by his strong sense of self-respect.

He marvelled at the way two strangers could hit it off, while there was such a gulf between some people who had lived together for years. He thought of Yuanyuan, Bamboo, Tian Shoucheng . . . and of Autumn's odd and ugly face.

They looked rather too refined for their rowdy surroundings. Between sips of *maotai** they ate slowly. At their age they had not much appetite. They smoked a good deal though and had plenty to say.

At the table on their right, some youngsters with flushed faces were noisily playing the guess-fingers game. Disturbing the whole restaurant. One of the waiters had to intervene.

The artist frowned. 'Chinese like a lively atmosphere when they eat.'

Zheng glanced round. 'Apart from the two of us, everyone here's young. Can't blame them. Eating out is their only diversion. What else can they do? They're bursting with energy. Dance? Out of the question. It's funny, in the fifties when dancing was fashionable, it didn't produce many hooligans. There's no culture worth speaking of, and

* A fiery white spirit.

nobody can afford to travel. I sympathize with them, but I can't help them. We ought to offer them better ways to let off steam.'

'You're right.'

'Why do some of us get so worked up about what young people want? Is it treason not to see eye to eye with us? Did we see eye to eye with our father's generation? The generation gap's wider than ever now. As dialectical materialists, we should acknowledge young people's right to change some of the things we approve of. We're too set in our ways. It's only natural for them to like what's new. Young people nowadays think for themselves. We should let them have their art exhibitions and stream of consciousness writing. They've more experience of life. Communists must forge ahead. If you're tired you can rest, but don't hold other people back.'

Zheng had drunk just enough to loosen his tongue and make him animated.

Yang Xiaodong eyed his thirteen mates. They were drinking and talking non-stop.

Some people were prejudiced against them and distrusted them, but they wanted to show what they were worth. Not that any of them would have said so, however, or admitted how moved he felt. They were too tough.

Yang opened a bottle of beer. As it frothed over he hastily filled their glasses. Then he raised his own and announced, 'Today we're celebrating the result of all of our efforts. So here's to us all!' He would have said more but his voice was trembling a little.

The rest stood up with their glasses. Wu Bin said, 'Hold on, we ought to have a picture!' He took a camera out of his satchel and told them where to stand.

'What about you?' asked Lü. 'Let's get someone else to take it.'

Zheng Ziyun was sitting at the next table. When Wu Bin looked round he met the vice-minister's eye.

'Will you take a picture of us?' he asked. 'Make sure

63

everyone's in the little frame, then press this button. This camera's automatic.'

Zheng readily agreed, wondering why they wanted a photograph. It wasn't a wedding – was it some reunion of distant friends? 'What's the occasion?' he asked.

Wu Bin told him, 'We're feeling good because this meal's our team's bonus!'

All fourteen of them clinked glasses and grinned broadly.

Yang Xiaodong proposed, 'Here's to the next time – next year!'

Zheng resumed his seat but kept looking towards their table.

Wu Bin called for silence, then rose to his feet. 'Let's drink one to Xiaodong. It's because we've got such a good boss that instead of being run down we've made it to the top. Drink up!'

Yang brushed this aside, refusing to stand up.

Zheng glanced with satisfaction at the artist.

Wu Bin urged, 'Look, we're all waiting for you. If you're too good to drink with us we'll stay standing here.'

Yang had to stand up and clink glasses. 'But you're wrong,' he demurred. 'It's not just my doing.'

Zheng asked Wu, 'Which factory are you from?'

'The Dawn Motor Works.'

'Why should a go-ahead team be run down?'

'According to our workshop boss we're a bunch of trouble-makers,' Lü Zhimin explained. 'Go-ahead? Not a hope! He's always finding fault!'

'Why talk about him?' objected Wu. 'I wouldn't work for *him*. But it's not his factory. The pay and the bonuses come from the state.'

'Officials don't seem very popular, do they?' the artist remarked with a twinkle to Zheng. 'Not even small officials. I wonder why.'

Zheng sipped his *maotai* and answered, 'Everyone comes in for some abuse. Even the emperors used to.' He turned to ask Lü, 'Why do you feel so strongly about your work-shop boss?'

64

'Even if we flog ourselves to death he always says we're a bad lot. Take Young Song here – ' He jerked his chin at a worried-looking young man and lowered his voice. 'He's a really good bloke. Found a girl friend for his brother. They went steady for a bit, then his brother lost interest in her. She invited him home to lunch on National Day, and the whole family waited till three o'clock but he didn't show up. Afterwards he kept avoiding her, pretending to be out. Young Song told him, "If you want to break with her, tell her. If you want to marry her and you're short of money I'll give you a few hundred."

'In the end the girl called it off. Young Song was so sorry for her, he proposed to her instead. But she felt she was too old for him, four years older. And we didn't like the idea either. In the end he talked her round. Then he consulted Xiaodong, our team leader – the one with the crew-cut there.

'Xiaodong said, "Do you want my advice, or are you telling me what you've decided? If your mind's made up, I'll back you. If you want my opinion, I'm dead against it."

'Young Song said, "I wasn't too keen at first, but since then we've really hit it off well, and my people are very fond of her too. The only trouble is that I don't get on with my brother any more."

'Xiaodong approved then, and told us all about it. He said that if there was any gossip outside we should silence it. Young Song's a good bloke, isn't he?'

'Yes indeed,' said Zheng. 'But why does he look so depressed?'

'He's got nowhere to live! We've still got to fix Song up with a room,' Lü called to Yang.

The others started joking about the difficulty of getting married. Zheng envied these lively youngsters. They could talk without inhibitions about love. As for him, he realized now he had never been in love.

He remembered Bamboo's response to his unromantic proposal of marriage. 'If that's what you need it's all right by me.' What need? Biological or spiritual? Neither, as it turned out.

Meanwhile Yang suggested a temporary solution for Song: partition off part of his parents' larger room, and apply for a room when their plant had new housing. As soon as they went back to work, they'd take two men off each shift to carry bricks while the rest covered for them. Everyone clapped their approval.

Song relaxed and felt much better now. Not just because of Yang's practical idea, but because his mates understood him and backed him up. Not like Wu Guodong's reaction to his request for a room: 'You in trouble then?'

Zheng asked, 'How does your workshop head run things?'

'Why don't you both move over here,' suggested Lü, 'instead of craning your necks.'

'How about it?' Zheng asked the artist, lowering his voice to add, 'They're from one of our ministry's motor works. I like them.'

'Of course,' chuckled the artist.

Wu Bin said, 'Our workshop head handles the work OK. He knows the ropes.'

'Could be a lot worse then,' commented Zheng.

Wu looked at him hard. Zheng struck him as a useless bookworm who knew nothing about factories. 'Production isn't everything,' he countered. 'He treats us like animals, like machines. But even animals need fodder, and machines have to be oiled.'

'Right on,' chimed in the painter.

'You're a good team.' Yang impressed Zheng as a young man who had been through the mill: sceptical, cool-headed, practical and able.

'We're nothing special,' said Yang, 'but we pull together.'

'How old are you?' asked the artist.

'Thirty-one.'

Wu Bin told him, 'It's not easy running a team in a works like ours. Not like being a minister who only has to sign documents. Anybody could do that.'

The artist grinned at Zheng. 'Hear that?'

Zheng kept a straight face. 'Just what my daughter thinks.'

'There's no mystery about it,' said Yang. 'All there is to it is keeping everyone happy. There are enough troubles in life without extra ones at work. We spend a third of our lives in that workshop and we ought to feel good there.'

Yang seldom talked so formally. Normally it would have embarrassed him to speak with such feeling. But with the beer, the chicken and the prawns today was special.

Lü said slowly to Zheng and the artist, 'I've never seen you before. Fact is, I'm the dumb one in our team; they're always bawling me out. But I like our team and I wouldn't leave it, because I feel good with my pals. Never mind all our other headaches. . .'

'There are enough of them,' put in Ge. 'Take the crammed buses for example. This morning the driver slammed on the brakes so hard that I was shoved and trod on a girl's heel. She glared at me and said, "Disgusting!" I ignored her. I don't row with girls. But I was fuming. Did she think she was so irresistible I'd done it on purpose?'

'We'd all much rather have our own motor-bikes than take the bus,' Lü continued. 'But on our lousy pay we can't afford one. Even if we had the money we couldn't get one. You have to queue up for everything. Even cabbage. Take housing. We're six in my family, three generations, and for twenty years we've lived in one ten-square-metre room . . .' Suddenly aware that he was depressing the others, he changed the subject. 'All I meant to say was, however many other headaches we have, we feel good in our team.'

The others were quiet, thinking.

'We're here to have a good time,' Yang reminded them. 'We're not like Minister Tian, who's all for revolutionary festivals. Come on, everybody tuck in.' He put a large piece of fish with his chopsticks on to the plate before Zheng. 'Go ahead, before it all gets cold.'

Ge remarked, 'If we put in another revolutionary Spring Festival we'd get enough overtime to pay for another binge.'

'Not worth it!' Wu Bin gulped down a whole glass of beer, then said contemptuously, 'Remember New Year's day in 1976 when he came to our plant to spend a revolutionary festival with the working masses? Wu Guodong begged and pleaded with us all to show up, so as not to make the leadership lose face. So we all got up at the crack of dawn, and Minister Tian didn't turn up till ten, with a woman in tow – who was she?'

'The head of some office in the ministry,' Yang told him.

'Some head!' Wu Bin snorted. 'They put on a cross-talk show, lectured us for an hour, then were off in a puff of smoke. All very well for him: he has a maid. Not like us. We need holidays to rest, visit our friends or do some washing and mending. What with the journey to and from work, the whole day was wasted. But he just piddled around in the factory for an hour, then got written up in the paper as a great revolutionary and took all the credit. That's the sort who get to the top. Hell! Is there any hope for China?'

Ge refilled his glass. 'Have a drink, never mind about him. You still get your pay.'

Wu would not drop the subject. 'With men like that in charge we'll never modernize. What do they care for the likes of us? Full pay but no rise in pay! If they were all like that there'd be no hope.'

The artist stealthily kicked Zheng under the table.

Zheng's expression had changed. He looked tired, old and withdrawn. He poured *maotai* for everyone and said, 'Let me drink to all you young comrades.'

Lü asked, 'What's the toast?'

'What's the toast?' Zheng turned to the artist who was watching him with a childish twinkle. 'I'm glad to be able to drink with you all today, and I hope we'll all succeed in our work. Here's to the next time. Drink up!'

All drained their glasses.

Wu Bin smacked his lips. 'Good stuff!'

As Lü shook hands with Zheng he asked, 'What do the two of you do?'

Buttoning his green padded army coat Zheng answered, 'He's an artist. I'm in administration.'

'Looking after eating, drinking, shitting, pissing and sleeping.'

'That's about it,' Zheng replied. 'That was a good meal, and well worth it.'

'It's made our workshop head livid!'

'Make him angrier still and he might see a bit of sense.'

As they stepped out of the restaurant the cold wind revived Zheng's flagging spirits. He walked the artist slowly to the bus stop. 'That meal was an eye-opener,' he said. 'That Yang Xiaodong has solved a problem for me. The way to get the workers keen isn't by learning from Daqing or empty talk, but by caring. That young fellow's a real psychologist. But I owe you an apology. I invited you to a meal, then made you listen to a lot of boring talk.'

'But it didn't bore me at all. They were saying what everyone thinks.'

'Oh?' Zheng stopped to stare at him.

'I was watching you all the time. I must draw your portrait. But you're a difficult subject. Your mood changes so fast. Changes every second.'

8

At a quarter to eight every morning, Tian Shoucheng, the Minister of Heavy Industry, walked unhurriedly into his office. Not like other ministers who turned up by car after eight. He made a point of this, and of passing the time of day with anyone he met in the corridor. He never seemed rushed.

Tian glanced at his outsize desk and the pile of papers on it, hung up his overcoat, smoothed his hair, made himself a mug of tea, then sat down to go through these documents and reports. Telegrams, Central Committee directives, a record of incoming phone calls, reports for him to minute . . . all were sorted out in order of importance.

Tian was more than satisfied with his secretary Xiao Yi. That he was thoroughly competent went without saying, and when heading one of the ministry's rebel contingents in the Cultural Revolution he had never gunned for Tian.

Tian signed the documents which needed signing, wrote comments on certain others.

He hesitated over an application for bonuses for the staff in the ministry hostel.

Recent editorials had called for strengthening political education and restricting bonuses to the equivalent of two months' pay. All factories were cutting down on them. So Tian wrote on the application. 'Handle in accordance with higher directives.' He liked the ambiguity of this.

He shrank from the bulky document next in the pile. Did the writer not know the unwritten rule that reports sent to the minister should be brief?

Frowning impatiently, he started to read it. It was a letter referred to him from above.

The letter criticized the Political Bureau's figure for the number of steel works, coal mines and oil fields to be in operation by the end of the century, saying that this was an ultra-Left approach to capital investment. The writer maintained that their investment was being over-extended, and funds and material were being wasted. Tian's heart sank. He sipped tea and sighed.

Since this letter had appeared on his desk, it must have been written in his ministry. He turned to the signature. Oh, Ho Jiabin, one of the rebels of the Cultural Revolution. Ho had written a poem and taken a wreath to Tiananmen Square in mourning for Premier Zhou in the spring of 1976 and would have ended up in prison if Commissioner Fang hadn't vouched for him. Why was he still stirring up trouble?

How to handle this? Tian twirled his pencil.

Finally he wrote, 'Refer to Vice-minister Zheng Ziyun.'

Fair enough. Zheng was keen on reforming industrial management and political work, opposed in fact to learning from Daqing. Tian looked on cynically as Zheng wasted his energy on such things as his opinion poll in the Dawn works. What nonsense! But he did not have to take him too seriously. Zheng already had plenty of enemies – virtually everyone with the old ideas.

An egg cracking against a rock!

Zheng had written an open letter to all the members of their Party branch, reporting Tian for spending nearly 200,000 yuan of public funds on building himself a fine house. Had said that Tian should make a public self-criticism and vacate some of the rooms for staff members with nowhere to live . . . And what had come of it? An investigation, and that was the end of that. After all it wasn't a matter of principle. It didn't involve the struggle between two lines.

Last year when Tian had been on a trip abroad he had sent Zheng to attend a conference called by the Central Committee in his place. Zheng had held forth on the need to make practice the criterion of truth, the need for an over-all scientific appraisal of Chairman Mao's writings instead of taking each word as gospel truth. And he had been dangerously premature in calling for the rehabilitation of Cultural Revolution victims.

Well, Tian knew that in politics you had to watch which way the wind was blowing. Everything else was hot air. Zheng wasn't likely to attend another such meeting.

Tian went to the outer office to return the speech Xiao Yi had written for him to deliver to a meeting of provincial commissioners. 'I've no specific faults to find,' he said. 'But it needs pulling together and rounding out. I don't want to sound too austere, but I don't want to be too lively either.'

Tian got others to write his speeches without telling them his own views. And he would make Xiao Yi sweat revising each speech many times for no apparent reason. His secretary listened, nodding his head, considering how to rehash the speech without actually changing the content. He knew that Tian would comment, 'Yes, this is much better.'

I've read these papers. Please pass them on to the appropriate people.'

Just then Lin Shaotong, another secretary, came in. Without a word he followed Tian into his office and closed the door behind him.

Xiao Yi went off to deliver the documents. He knew they never wanted him to overhear them, and he himself wanted nothing to do with them. There was something wrong and unprincipled about their close relationship, reminiscent of the cliques in the Cultural Revolution. He too had done many senseless things then, caught up in the general hysteria. Now he was cured, apathetic. But he saw something of the manoeuvring which went on behind the scenes.

Ji delivered Ho Jiabin's letter to Vice-minister Zheng. 'This is from Minister Tian!'

Zheng scanned it quickly, then with a glance at Ji stuffed it into a drawer of his desk. 'All right.'

Ji knew that Zheng agreed with what Ho had written in his letter.

When Ji had left Zheng read the letter carefully, nodding from time to time. Then he dropped it on the desk as if it were too hot to handle.

He knew he could never have written such an exposure to his seniors, clearly stating his true views. Had worldly considerations made him lose his integrity?

After his return from the cadre school* he had not seen Ho Jiabin for a long time. While under investigation they had worked in the same team. Ho often took on jobs that were too much for Zheng, and liked to discuss all sorts of questions with him. Zheng always felt younger in his company. Ho kept up his spirits by cracking caustic jokes, telling him such things as the nickname of the head of their study group: the Mad Piano.

Once back in the ministry in their different posts they

* Following Mao Zedong's 'May 7th directive' of 1966, China's professional and university trained personnel were sent to the countryside to re-educate in cadre schools. At least twenty million people underwent this experience.

72

had drifted apart. Work, endless work kept Zheng busy. He ought to have a talk with Ho, if not about this letter, then about old times. Autumn had told him she and Ho meant to collaborate on writing up Chen Yongming, a factory manager with the guts to go all out for modernization. Autumn struck him as slightly unbalanced, one day studying the reform of the economic system, the next writing reportage. No doubt writers had these sudden crazes. Zheng picked up the phone to ask Ho over for a chat, but then thought better of it. He deliberately kept at a distance from his colleagues, afraid that too close a relationship would make it hard to stick to principles, might cause misunderstanding.

But what about that letter? The minister was obviously passing the buck again. Things were still very complex, with a struggle raging between the reformers and those set in the old ways. All the sloganeers had ganged up together. Regardless of objective possibilities and the burden on the people, they demanded huge sums from the state and set impossible economic targets. If the mistakes of the Big Leap were repeated, the country would soon go bust. And one of the main factors obstructing reform was that the old guard clung stubbornly to their power.

What else was production for under socialism unless to make the country rich and strong. But had they achieved this? No. Their planning took too little account of objective needs and put too much stress on heavy industry.

The feasibility of projects was never scientifically analyzed.

Industrial management was still old-fashioned, with no scientific methods, plans or budget. Individuals simply shouted slogans and issued orders to complete a project by a certain time. The result was naturally chaos.

Hot air and lies had become the order of the day . . .

The situation was complicated and difficult. For this struggle was not against the enemy. It was against comrades whose wrongheaded ideas had plunged the people into poverty and given rise to countless social problems. Hence the despair and pessimism.

In a socialist country the people couldn't be made to go on living this way. Zheng pounded his desk.

He put Ho's letter into his bottom drawer. Letter-writers who exposed problems should be protected, not have their letters sent back to their organization. Comrades like Ho Jiabin were all too few.

'What is it?' Minister Tian asked his crony Lin.

'Young Ji told me this morning Vice-minister Zheng and Vice-minister Wang went to B — University yesterday to see Professor Dai.'

'Oh?' Tian was taken aback.

Why should two communist ministers take it into their heads to call on a bourgeois professor? A notorious Rightist, only just cleared. No wonder there had recently been talk about two rival headquarters in their ministry. Like the Cultural Revolution all over again.

'What did they talk about?'

'I don't know. They didn't take their secretaries. My guess is it had something to do with the coming forum on political work.'

'Didn't I say at the last Party meeting that forum was postponed? We're not ready for it.'

Tian invariably used delaying tactics.

But apparently Zheng and Wang meant to go ahead.

'According to our research staff they want to find out more about sociology and psychology. The idea is to make political work more scientific.'

Tian gaped.

Zheng and Wang kept hobnobbing with professors, writers and reporters, making speeches and writing articles to build up their reputation. All through history writers had made trouble. Tian felt a vague foreboding.

Psychology had long been denounced as a bourgeois pseudo-science. It was right to arouse the workers' enthusiasm, but psychology was not the way to do it. But as everyone was going on about improving industrial management he as a minister would have to make some

74

proposals too. They could also keep Wang and Zheng under control.

'I've been considering merging the management and research offices into an advisory committee to study this question,' he said.

That would mean removing the research office from Wang Fangliang's control and setting up an opposition group. But Wang was shrewd, had drive, and had backing too. Better not cross swords with him over a minor issue.

Wang and Zheng were not close friends, yet in Party discussions they sided with each other. Tian had noticed that Zheng did not make friends or let others know what he was thinking. He and Wang must need each other's help. What for? Were they cooking something up?

'That reporter Ye Zhiqiu on the phone again,' Ji Hengquan told Zheng.

Zheng frowned. It was imprudent of Autumn to keep ringing up and calling him Old Zheng instead of Comrade Zheng Ziyun. She should know that at least a dozen people listened to his telephone calls. And she kept writing to him about social problems. Her humorous, informal notes were a treat to read. However, in China so steeped in feudal ideas people took an exaggerated interest in women, and he must be careful of his reputation.

Zheng received many letters every day, which Ji read through for him, even if the envelope was labelled 'Personal'. Ji always answered the phone too. Autumn's casual calls and notes could easily be misconstrued. His secretary announced her calls with a conspiratorial air. It was infuriating.

Should he ask Autumn to write to him at home? No, that would look as if there really were something between them. Besides, he sensed Autumn's aversion to Bamboo and did not want to exacerbate it. After all, Bamboo was his wife. They were generally considered a 'model couple'.

Zheng picked up the receiver and said formally, 'Zheng Ziyun speaking. How are you?'

Autumn came straight to the point. 'I've some bad news for you. Your article on political work isn't going to be printed the day after tomorrow.'

'Why not? The editor told me it would be.' Zheng felt rather exasperated. The paper had commissioned this article.

'It was decided higher up. They hope you'll reconsider some of your formulations.'

'Which? Can't you be more specific?'

'Like "group consciousness". We usually use "collectivism".' Autumn laughed. 'I see no need to change it. You should stick to it. Our political departments don't understand why their work should be more scientific. And to them psychology and sociology are bourgeois. Did you read that report on management in the Toyota car plant in Japan? More effective than ours, I think. If there's a death in a worker's family, the management pays for the funeral; if anyone has a birthday, they give him a present – that's psychologically sound. Of course their aim is to make money for the bosses, but why shouldn't we use the same methods for socialism?'

Autumn was defending his article as stoutly as if she had written it herself.

Zheng's sole remaining ambition was to use his lifetime's experience to reform industrial management in this new period. This article was the first of a series he was writing on the subject. If he refused to revise it they might not publish the rest.

Autumn lowered her voice, disappointed by his reaction. 'Mind you, they may agree not to make any changes, then bring it out altered out of all recognition. You'd better bear that in mind. If they won't print it as it stands, why not send a copy to the Central Committee? I think those new ideas of yours most important.'

'Thank you, we'll discuss that later.' Zheng rang off. No one in the ministry talked to him like that, overstepping the limits.

Limits came in useful to hide things you lacked the courage to face.

The sun slanting through the window dazzled his eyes. He leant back in his chair.

He had nothing very demanding to do that day, no interminable meetings. Yet he felt tired. Or rather depressed by his own lack of courage.

Very well then, another compromise. He was powerless to change the situation.

Perhaps this was partly why he had rung off so quickly, to avoid Autumn's reproach: Why not stick to your guns? She might not say this but would surely think it.

An individual's character does not always correspond to his position. Autumn always made Zheng conscious of his deficiencies. Some strange quality about her impelled others to want to show her their best side.

9

Chen Yongming was worn out. The nearby gongs and drums, the cheerful din of voices and fire-crackers, sounded faint and far away.

All the families granted housing had invited him to eat dumplings. These were now boiling in the construction team's big pan. Chen disliked such commotion but did not want to spoil their enjoyment, to which his presence was contributing.

He had slept very little in the last few days, during which Lü Zhimin had been fighting for his life.

Young Lü had fallen off the scaffolding while painting a drainpipe. Entirely due to his own negligence.

But Chen took the blame on himself. He should have foreseen that as the construction neared completion the workers would grow careless. Should have warned them to be on their guard.

He spent hours on a bench outside the operating theatre. Each time a white-coated doctor came out, his heart missed a beat. Even when Radiance came to sit beside him he turned away from her, simply asking, 'How is he?'

'It's serious, a ruptured liver. . .'

'Any hope?'

'We're doing our best.'

'Right, back to your work.'

Only when Lü Zhimin was out of danger did Chen rest his head on Radiance's soft shoulder.

A red silk banner was flapping in the wind. Unaccountably the sight brought tears to Chen's eyes. Was this because of Young Lü's recovery? Or because the workers were all so overjoyed?

Rows of very simple housing. But homes they had longed for for years.

In hospital Lü had said, 'Young Song, you move in. We're good mates. Since that room was given to me, I can make it over. The manager says we'll be building more; it's only a matter of time.'

How would they react, those bureaucrats in high-rise buildings who paid lip-service to 'class feeling', if they heard Lü Zhimin's proposal and saw the wild rejoicing of the workers over such simple housing?

When the dumplings were ready, Li Ruilin elbowed his way through the crowd. 'You must let me give these to Old Chen,' he said.

Some time ago Chen had given Li the job of making a pond in which to breed fish for the workers. He had stressed that the coffer-dam should be firmly tamped down, then covered with stones, with a layer of sand on top. Li, still angry with him, had resented these instructions and failed to carry them out. As a result, when the fingerlings had been put into the pond and the water froze, the coffer-dam had cracked, letting out the water and fish. Li realized this spelt trouble. The whole plant had such high hopes of their poultry farm and fishpond, since prices were going up so fast outside. He went to Chen's office and wept. Chen was angry, but after a silence he said:

'Don't be so cut up, Old Li. I'll help you rebuild it.'

'Bawl me out!'

'Why? I can see you've taken it to heart. That shows a strong sense of responsibility – fine.'

Li got over his resentment at his demotion. He looked at Chen and all he had done with new eyes.

The smell of the dumplings nauseated Chen. He had no appetite, he would have liked to sleep for three whole days on end. But he knew that was out of the question. He had just been summoned by the ministry to a meeting on political work, at which he would have to make a speech. The notice was worded in a curious way. It called both for learning from Daqing in political work and also going about it more scientifically. That sounded contradictory. Well, he would stick to his guns and summarize his own experience.

Vice-minister Zheng Ziyun had also rung up saying that tomorrow, Sunday, he would be coming to the plant. In order to give his driver a day off he wanted Chen to fetch him. He had not told his secretary, not wishing to be accompanied by a whole retinue of commissioners, section chiefs, engineers and technicians. Chen wondered why he was coming.

After taking the bowl of dumplings Chen said gruffly, 'Thanks! Thank you all.' But his hand was too unsteady to pick one up with the chopsticks until the third attempt. He looked round. A hush had fallen. Everyone present was watching him in silence. The sight gave him fresh strength. Old Lü's bearded chin beneath his bleary eyes was quivering. Chen put the dumpling into the old fellow's mouth. 'I let you down, Old Lü,' he said.

Old Lü, tears running down his cheeks, ate the dumpling. 'Don't give me that sort of talk, Old Chen!'

Chen shouted, 'Beat the drums!'

At once the drummers sounded a rousing tattoo.

As it was known that Chen Yongming had been recommended by Zheng Ziyun to manage the Dawn Motor

Works, Feng Xiaoxian wrote Zheng a letter. Feng had headed this motor works himself in the time of the Gang of Four, and of course no one could blame him for not doing a good job in those days. Now he envied Chen's success. This was what he wrote:

> Comrade Ziyun,
> How are you? Two middle-ranking cadres in the Dawn Motor Works have written me a letter which they want referred to Minister Tian. They have heard that our ministry and certain papers mean to praise their factory's management, and they are dead against this. The plant has made some progress but still has many problems: the workers and middle management are disgruntled, and production is not going up. They're heavily in debt and overstaffed. They're trying to buy popularity with welfare benefits and paying more attention to living conditions than to production. While illicitly building housing for their workers, they had a very serious accident. They have cooked their accounts as well, charging their housing to their capital account, and have disbanded their political department and the Daqing office. The middle-rank cadres don't want to work there, and the workers are full of gripes. So if the management is praised that will only increase the general dissatisfaction. When a young worker called Yang was written up in the press it caused a storm of protest.
> As I don't know the facts, I can only refer this letter to Minister Tian. Please report to him on this at your earliest convenience.
> Greetings,
> Feng Xiaoxian

Feng struck Zheng as a man who would never achieve much but would never make big trouble either. Political departments were packed with such cadres, in the mistaken belief that their lack of technical know-how would not affect the work of other sections.

Such men simply wanted to get by – what political work could they do? Most of them had forgotten the meaning of the word.

But evidently he had underestimated Feng. The fellow was not so simple.

On the basis of this letter the ministry's Party Committee had decided against commending Chen Yongming. Ridiculous! What right had they to ban the publication of such articles? They should have investigated the charges made in the letter first. It was irresponsible to condemn a comrade out of hand like that.

Zheng Ziyun went first to the canteen, where he knew he would find things not to be seen in the imposing front buildings. The cooks were carefully seasoning the vegetables. They obviously took pride in their work. Not like some cooks who boiled up a pan of cabbage as if preparing pigs' swill.

The nursery was fairly well run too. At the head of each cot was a picture of an animal: Mother Bear in a red skirt toasting flap-jacks; a white rabbit in a blue vest holding a big carrot; a fox stealing grapes . . . they reminded him of the stories told him in childhood. Smiling he tried sitting on one of the little chairs, then stood up shaking his head.

Chen's bloodshot eyes widened as if with disapproval. Zheng patted him on the back. 'You're worn out, that's made you edgy.'

Next they visited the new housing, which already looked thoroughly lived in. On the small balconies hung ragged quilts and clothes of different colours, above stacks of junk and scraps of building material left over from earthquake shelters.

Zheng had visited many factories. To get to know one was like getting to know a person: you couldn't rely on hearsay. In the workshops you could feel the pulse of the whole plant. He also had to admit that Chen could reel off the figures on output, profit and so on without consulting a notebook. More than could be said of most factory managers.

Work was going with a steady rhythm. No one was chatting, reading a paper, strolling around or napping. Zheng noticed a turner and a milling machine operator carefully inspecting a processed part and filling up a mimeographed progress sheet. 'Do they all fill these up?' he asked Chen.

'Yes. Each workshop, team and worker has a mandatory production quota. Strict records are kept, so everybody has to complete his quota. And if anything is missing, we check up on where it went. That applies from the delivery of raw materials down to the finished product. We have accurate figures on the number of finished products, the number of rejects. This makes everyone feel more responsible, and he knows if he's done his day's quota.'

Zheng nodded. 'How do you assign bonuses?'

'When bonuses were approved in July 1978, everyone was very pleased at first. But the problem was how to distribute bonuses fairly. As we had no set quality standards and no figures were available there were endless squabbles. No one was satisfied. That forced us to change our management methods. The team heads had to have a way of knowing who'd done the best work and in what way. So we set standards and announced everyone's figures every month. That showed who deserved a bonus. No meetings needed and no more squabbles.

'We also made a rule that if you fail to fulfil your quota without good reason, you lose 5 to 15 per cent of your wages.'

'Did no one object?'

'Sure. Some said, "You've no right to dock my pay." I asked, "What right have you not to complete your quota?"'

'And the factory approved this?' Zheng was amazed by Chen's nerve.

'We made other provisions so that if there's a valid reason for not completing the quota it can be proved. If a lathe breaks down, the repair team signs an equipment repair chit to prove it. The clinic signs for sick leave. And it's a matter of self-respect for the workers to finish their

82

quota. So far there have been no complaints to the Party committee. If you double your permitted reject rate your pay is docked; but if a man puts in overtime to bring the ratio down, he's not penalized.'

'What about electricians, maintenance men, office staff? How do you motivate them?'

Chen realized that Zheng knew what he was talking about and was keenly interested, so he answered his questions patiently and in detail. The maintenance men, for example, got bonuses depending on how little time the machines for which they were responsible were out of action.

A basketball slammed into Zheng's heel, nearly knocking him over. Looking round he saw some players grinning sheepishly. His eyes met those of Wu Bin who was running over to retrieve the ball. The young fellow halted and gaped at seeing Zheng being shown round by their manager – he must be someone high up in the ministry.

Zheng held out his hand with a smile. 'How are you? Remember me?'

Wu Bin's hand, grimy and sweaty, clasped Zheng's firmly. 'Of course.' He turned and whistled. The other players ran over – the team that had eaten in the New Wind Restaurant.

'Have you met before?' Chen was surprised.

Zheng explained briefly, then told Yang, 'I was looking for you.'

'For me?' This puzzled Yang.

'Yes, the ministry's going to hold a forum on political work. I want you to come and tell them about how you do things.'

Chen laughed. 'You've found the right man.'

Yang said nervously, 'You must be kidding. I'm not even a Party member. I can't talk about political work. Better ask our workshop head Wu Guodong.'

'The man you were being so uncomplimentary about that day?'

'Yes,' chimed in Wu Bin. 'He's a dab at meetings. He went to the ministry's first meeting on learning from Daqing. Gave a speech in the stadium about what he'd earned from it. Had a slap-up meal, stayed in a posh hostel, and met top government people. Our plant didn't half crack him up! He has the gift of the gab, won't put his foot in it.'

Zheng told Chen, 'Hear that? A criticism of you!'

'And of the ministry too,' Chen retorted.

Yang objected, 'Besides, I wouldn't know what to say.'

'Just repeat what you said in the restaurant that day,' Zheng told him. 'I'd like Comrade Wu Bin to come too.'

With that he walked over to the parking lot where new trucks were lined up. The youngsters followed. They were not overawed by his status as he made a good impression on them.

Zheng opened the door of the front truck and ran a finger over the driver's seat, leaving a line in the dust. 'Not airtight,' he commented. 'What's its fuel consumption?'

'Fifteen or sixteen litres for a hundred kilometres.'*

'The Japanese equivalent would do it on twelve or thirteen,' remarked Zheng. He knew this plant was not solely responsible, as many of the components were manufactured else-where.

He climbed into the cabin. 'Anyone willing to risk a ride with me?' Chen didn't stop him, knowing that he could drive.

Wu Bin hopped in. He liked Zheng because he was reasonable and practical, not the type of bureaucrat who just sat in his office signing papers. Besides, he wanted to be there to help in case the old fellow couldn't cope.

Zheng's foot in a cloth shoe and brown woollen sock pressed down steadily. The engine started. Good, he knew what he was doing. He backed out of the parking lot on to the asphalt drive.

'Where's Young Lü today?' he asked.

---

* About twenty-three miles to the gallon.

84

'He had an accident when we were building our housing. He's in hospital.'

'What was the general reaction?'

Wu Bin glanced at him but said nothing. Zheng sensed the gap between them widening. He smiled, realizing Wu Bin's loyalty to Chen.

'Some people gloated,' Wu Bin finally told him. 'Mostly bureaucrats. The rest of us understood.'

'The acceleration's not very lively.' Zheng changed the subject.

Not until lighting-up time did Chen take Zheng back to the city. As they were both too tired to talk, Chen put on a cassette.

'Chopin's 2nd Piano Concerto in F Minor,' remarked Zheng.

Keeping his eyes on the dark road, Chen said slowly, 'In middle school I was mad on the violin, thought music the highest form of art. And I wanted to get a PhD in physics. But I've ended up a factory manager!" He laughed rather bitterly.

Zheng remained silent. So much wasted effort in their lives.

Suddenly Chen pulled up by the roadside and opened the door. The air held a tang of spring, a reminder that trees were burgeoning, grass growing again and insects stirring after hibernation. There would soon be thunder and rain.

The two men got out and looked up at the sky. It was a black moonless night.

Chen said grimly, 'People are gunning for me for going too far, building housing for the workers instead of turning all our profits in to the state. I've set up a poultry farm and fishpond too. The accounts were a shambles before, but no one checked up on the previous managers. They squandered hundreds of millions of yuan, but I just spent two million on workers' housing. If they sue me, I'm positive I can win my case. Besides, all factories are doing it. I've paid our profit to the state and more. Why shouldn't I juggle some funds to solve the factory's biggest problem?'

Zheng said nothing. Chen needed not sympathy but support and understanding. He wasn't worried about him, knew he would stick it out.

'They accuse me of courting popularity,' Chen went on, 'call me a welfare manager – so much the better. The fools! To boost production in China you have to improve living conditions. They blame me for disbanding the Daqing Office and the Political Section. China has hundreds of thousands of enterprises, each one different, and if we all do things the Daqing way we'll never up our output or feed our workers.' He hurled his half-smoked cigarette to the ground, sending sparks flying through the dark. Then calming down he said, 'You must be hungry, just listening to me grumbling. Come home for supper with us. I've some good liquor.'

'Grumble away. Get it off your chest. I'll back you up, Chen. Not that I carry much weight. I'm always bashing my head against brick walls. In fact, I've plenty to gripe about myself.'

When Chen opened the door of his flat, they heard the sound of frying.

Walking in behind Chen, Zheng heard a woman remonstrate fondly, 'Late again.' He saw a green-sleeved arm thrown round Chen's neck. Heard the sound of a kiss. To think that a Chinese factory manager had such foreign habits! Not that there was such a difference between Chinese and foreigners behind closed doors. Zheng smiled. Chen and his wife must be very close.

As Chen stepped aside the light fell on Zheng. At once Radiance covered her face with her floury hands and gave an exclamation of dismay. She flashed a reproachful glance at her husband for not telling her they had a visitor.

To save her embarrassment and conceal his status, Zheng introduced himself, 'I'm Zheng.'

To go with their drinks they had a dish of fried peanuts. The meat-stuffed pancakes were piping hot, done to a turn. And there was thick millet gruel. It was a long time since

Zheng had last eaten this. The meal warmed him up. The cramped two-room flat felt comfortably lived in, unlike his cold empty home. Radiance's peaceful charm seemed to ease away all irritations.

He did not get home till after eight. His chest felt constricted after his tiring day, but he spread out a sheet of paper and wrote:

Comrade Feng Xiaoxian,

Many thanks for your letter. I was glad to learn the views of those two comrades in the Dawn Motor Works.

Comrade Chen Yongming worked for many years in our ministry. When the Gang of Four was rampant he had the guts to oppose their line. Since taking charge of the Dawn Motor Works he has tackled difficult problems.

The Motor Works' debts, its redundant staff and the poor quality of its products are the legacy of the past, not Chen's responsibility.

Those in leading positions must unite with the cadres and workers to overcome the many problems that face us, and this can't be done overnight.

I hope you will pass this letter on to the two cadres who wrote to you. If they have more to say, they can write to me directly and we can discuss the question at greater length.

Greetings!

Zheng Ziyun

A stabbing pain in his back. His heart was playing up. Zheng had to be fit and strong. He still had more to do in life; his successors needed more time to prepare themselves properly.

Not one paper had yet been written on enterprise management for the annual conference of the National Association for Management Studies. Zheng had in mind a twelve-point proposal for the way the Ministry of Heavy

Industry should develop. He meant to produce a first draft in May, try it out for reactions in June, then revise it. He could finalize it that autumn and have it printed by the end of the year as a manual for industrial modernization.

The management of China's state-owned enterprises was still like that of handicrafts. This had to change. Ideological work had got to be more scientific. At the forthcoming forum they must invite economists, psychologists, sociologists and behaviourists, as well as cadres doing political work. This was what Autumn had proposed, but his article had been axed. Zheng felt frustrated.

The watch under his pillow was ticking loudly. He pulled it out and flung it to the foot of the bed.

10

Early summer. The noon break was now two hours. Mo Zheng would have preferred a shorter rest after lunch, so as to go home earlier in the evenings. He longed to get back to his little room where he was surrounded by friends: his music, his books. How was it that he felt so at home with writers who had lived so long ago, so far from today's society?

In real life people had different standards of judgement.

Their team leader Su had lost his wallet. The other team members had suspected Mo Zheng and gossiped behind his back, breaking off when he came within hearing. Some gave hair-raising accounts of robberies, adding grimly that no matter how crafty the thief he would be brought to justice, and directing menacing glances at Mo Zheng.

Today the wallet had been found in the team leader's home. Everyone had roared with laughter, and no one had shown the least compunction for having suspected Mo Zheng.

True, he had once stolen. But they knew what had driven him to it. And that was over and done with.

Mo Zheng sat on the grass fiddling with his pruning shears, thinking how much more care was taken of growing trees than had ever been given to him. Autumn cared about him, but not even her rocklike shoulders could carry the pressure of social prejudice which weighed so heavily on him.

With a sigh he put down the shears, took off his jacket, spread it out and lay down.

The foliage was already luxuriant. There was a pervasive smell of cool, moist soil. When he turned his head grass caressed his bronzed cheeks.

At least the grass and sunlight gave him the same fragrance and warmth as to other people.

White clouds drifted across the blue sky. A bird was circling far away. The breeze lulled him to sleep.

He was short of sleep. He was reading a chapter of *Les Misérables* before bed every night so as to be able to tell Yuanyuan about it.

Autumn had urged him to do this to keep up his French.

He had objected, 'Why should I? I'm not going to take the university entrance exams.'

'Is that any excuse for wasting your life? You ought to educate yourself. If you have intellectual interests, life won't get you down.'

Autumn herself often turned to literature when frustrated.

Mo Zheng thought her advice childish, like telling someone with a broken leg to put mercurochrome on it.

But then Yuanyuan had made him change his mind.

When he came off work that day, he heard a girl's sweet, soft voice that stopped him in his tracks. He was afraid to make a sound that might frighten her away.

She was saying, 'Why should a bishop like Myriel be so broad-minded when a lot of so-called Marxists have so many prejudices? Not just prejudices, metaphysical notions! What a shame that nobody's translated the rest of that novel. I'd love to know how it ends.'

Her voice had a candour after his own heart.

Autumn replied, 'I could ask Mo Zheng to read it to you.

He has a copy of it in French, but he's grown very lazy. When I urge him to keep up his French, he pays no attention. Goodness knows how he spends his time lying in his little room.'

'Who's Mo Zheng? Your son?'

'No, I have no son. He's a young friend. I wonder if he's back.' She called, 'Mo Zheng!'

He panicked. He wanted to see this girl. But what could he say to her?

She was no breath-taking beauty, yet Mo Zheng felt thrown off balance. Cruel fate put such a girl beyond his reach.

She held out her hand. 'I'm Zheng Yuanyuan. I don't like the name, but I can't think of a better one.'

Her hand was so small he was afraid to grip it for fear of hurting her.

Yuanyuan sat down on the stool which Autumn had urged him to throw out. It tilted backwards and she toppled off it. Mo Zheng sprang forward and steadied her just in time.

Autumn scolded, 'I told you to chuck that stool out.'

'You must be a good volley-ball player,' Yuanyuan remarked.

Mo Zheng stood there woodenly, unable to answer.

'Will you tell me the rest of the story?' She was looking up at him with wilful eyes, which he found irresistible.

He answered helplessly, 'You may be disappointed.'

'I'll come over at half past seven every evening.' Yuanyuan wondered why she was bossing a stranger like this. She had never behaved this way to other young men. Botheration! Had she been too flighty? She pulled a long face and turning her back on him said coldly to Autumn, 'I must go now.'

Her departure seemed to lower the temperature. Mo Zheng took the stool she had sat on back to his room.

He paced up and down until Autumn called out, 'Aren't you going to sleep, Mo Zheng? Take off your boots at least. You sound like a column of tanks.'

How long was it since he had done anything conscientiously? He looked up dictionaries, grammars . . . To have those wilful eyes gazing at him, he wished he were a writer or translator.

It was only by luck that he had kept this book. When his parents had been cleared posthumously and their belongings returned to him, he had just picked out this copy of *Les Misérables*. Perhaps it was because his mother had read it to him when he was a child, and it had left a deep impression on him. He loved Jean Valjean because in spite of all his sufferings he had retained his humanity. Was this because he identified himself with Jean Valjean?

As he read the novel to Yuanyuan he watched her reactions. Did she love Jean Valjean too or simply sympathize with him? But what was that to him? Would she act in the same way towards him if she knew about his past? Jean Valjean was a fictitious character. But his past was enough to frighten off any girl conventionally brought up.

Mo Zheng even envied Victor Hugo. Although he'd lived over a century ago the old man had brought tears to Yuanyuan's adorable eyes. Mo Zheng felt himself falling into an abyss. Already deprived of so much, if he lost his love that would be the end of him.

None of this escaped Autumn's sharp eyes. Herself childless, her maternal love for Mo Zheng made her worry about him. She regretted initiating these reading sessions, which might have a tragic conclusion. Even if Yuanyuan threw caution to the winds, her parents would never agree to such a marriage. Was the girl strong enough to defy them? For Mo Zheng's sake she must put a stop to their friendship. She asked Yuanyuan:

'Do you know who Mo Zheng's like?'

The girl wouldn't give herself away by answering.

'He's like Jean Valjean!'

'Oh!' Yuanyuan's reaction was ambiguous. Did it express disagreement, surprise or regret?

'Do you know what I mean?'

'What do you mean?' Another evasive answer.

'It means he'd better forget about love.'

'Really?' Yuanyuan was leafing through a pictorial, too upset to sit still for fear she would burst into tears. Autumn seemed to be implying that she was flirting with Mo Zheng. This was more than she could bear.

When Yuanyuan left her heart ached for Mo Zheng. Tears coursed down her cheeks. Did she love him? She didn't know. She liked to have him at her beck and call. Felt possessive about him. But was that love? What was lovable about him? He could never go to university, never grow rich, perhaps never join the Party. He never expressed fine sentiments, but when Granny Wang upstairs had a stroke he had nursed her in the hospital till her son came back from Xinjiang – the doctors had all taken him for her grandson. He had freed a lovely little bird which had flown into his room . . . Was that all? Well, to Yuanyuan it meant a lot.

What a silly girl she was!

Her sister's husband was a research student in economics. Yuanyuan had read his thesis, filled with quotations from the Marxist classics but expressing no original ideas. He practically knew the whole of Marx and Engels by heart. Dad had commented, 'He learns by rote, the way I memorized the Chinese classics.' Yuanyuan found her brother-in-law ridiculous. All he had learned from his study of economics was how to take advantage of other people. He was even more calculating than her mother. The thought of such a man as a husband made her feel sick.

Her parents were well-off, but were they happy? They never talked to each other from the heart. Never stood side by side at the window to watch falling leaves in the rain. Just tried to score off each other.

On the subject of Party members, Yuanyuan was less prejudiced than some young people who exclaimed contemptuously, 'Join the Party? What for?' Still, she didn't consider Party membership the sole criterion for judging character.

Did she pity Mo Zheng, or did she love him? Love wasn't

a question of charity, it was the feeling that you couldn't live without someone. Did she really need him? Autumn had intimated that if she let him love her, then turned him down, that would kill him.

For ten days on end she tortured herself.

Autumn saw that Mo Zheng was losing weight, had grown more silent, stopped reading or playing the piano. Still, she believed she had done the right thing by him, and he would get over it. At the same time she felt disappointed with Yuanyuan, just as she sometimes did with Zheng Ziyun. Why hadn't he put up a fight to get that brilliant article of his published?

Every evening after supper Mo Zheng skulked in his room, his ears pricked up to listen for footsteps on the stairs. By ten o'clock, when it was too late for her to come, he started looking forward to the next evening. He had often known despair, but this time it was harder to endure.

He couldn't go to seek her; he could only wait passively. If he hadn't been in Jean Valjean's position, he could have fought for her, could have won her love. Now, however, all he could do was wonder whether she had been playing with him. She didn't seem a flirt. She'd admitted to him, 'I've been lying again.'

'Lying?' He couldn't keep up with her changing moods.

'Yes. Mum asked me, "Where do you fool about every evening?" She emphasized "fool about", her expression stern. I told her, "I'm learning French." So you'll have to teach me a few phrases.'

Was this a tacit pact? A love pact?

She must realize how he felt. Their relationship gave him no right to ask anything of her. He could only accept her love if she offered it, not out of pity but out of respect. As a child Mo Zheng had heard his mother pray to the Virgin Mary. For him there was no Virgin Mary, only Yuanyuan.

But did she understand that he was Jean Valjean?

There came no knock at the door.

Mo Zheng despaired.

Yuanyuan's face when she came was clouded, disturbing Autumn. Never having been in love herself, she couldn't understand lovers. But she knew she should stay in her own room, both happy and worried for them.

Yuanyuan turned away sulkily, her lovely bobbed hair close to Mo Zheng's lips. 'I've something to tell you,' he said.

'No need!' She whirled round and flared up. 'How selfish you are, just thinking of yourself!'

A girl would only say such a thing to a man she considered her own.

But she was really angry. Despite her concern for Mo Zheng, she resented having to make the first overtures.

That was because she considered him her equal.

In what way had he been selfish? Mo Zheng had no idea. 'What do you want . . .' he stammered.

Yuanyuan sat down on the sofa and said softly, 'I want something to eat and I'm thirsty.' No need to explain that all these days she had lost her appetite.

Where was the tin of cakes? He couldn't see it.

'Stupid!' Yuanyuan stamped her feet. 'There it is, on top of the bookcase.'

Making coffee, he scalded his hand. At once Yuanyuan took it, asking, 'Does it hurt?' No one had ever shown such concern for him!

Mo Zheng's eyes misted over.

'It hurts here,' he said gruffly, and laid her hand on his chest.

She sighed. 'My fault.' She lowered her eyes.

'No, I don't know how to thank you.'

Yuanyuan felt his hot breath on her hair. Afraid to look up, she stared at the top black button on his jacket and the thick blue thread with which he had sewn it on. That thread seemed to proclaim what a lonely, frustrated life he led. Slowly she withdrew her hand from his and fingered the button wondering: Is he watching me? Waiting for me to speak? . . .

Mo Zheng seized her hand and carried it to his lips. After a hurried kiss he let it go. He picked up the steaming coffee, stirred it with a teaspoon, blew on it, then handed it to Yuanyuan. 'Watch out, it's still hot.' This was spoken as casually as if nothing had happened.

Yuanyuan felt rather let down. She glanced at his jet black eyes. What had come over him, making him so unlike his usual intractable self?

Mo Zheng knew this was a dream. He ought to wake up but was powerless to do so.

She turned away.

'Yuanyuan!' he pleaded.

'Well?'

'Where are you going?'

'To see dad. He's speaking at a meeting in the ministry today. I'm afraid the strain may be too much for his heart. He wants me to go and listen. He calls me an ignoramus. Says while I'm young and still have a good memory, I should learn more about our society.'

Though Mo Zheng had never met Zheng Ziyun or taken any interest in him he realized now that his own view of society might be too one-sided. There were people at all levels who worked hard. Not all high officials rested on their laurels.

The meeting-hall was not large. Zheng's spirits rose when he saw his daughter slip in and sit beside Autumn. She cared about his health, his morale, his work. When she left to get married, his home would have no further attraction for him. What sort of man would she marry? He expected her to spring a bombshell on him and Bamboo. Her recent behaviour had been rather secretive. Was she in love? He wouldn't ask her. He never read her letters or diary. And he had tried to stop Bamboo from searching her room. 'This comes of your bourgeois education in a mission school,' she had sneered. 'Have you any letters you don't want me to read?'

So he had advised Yuanyuan to put a lock on her drawer. The two of them saw eye to eye on family matters.

Wang Fangliang was making the opening speech, stressing that modernization was their main political task.

Zheng glanced round to note listeners' reactions. His eyes met those of Yang Xiaodong, whose face was expressionless. Zheng winked at him and Yang nodded back politely. Yang was not the lively youngster he had been in the restaurant.

'. . . Because of the ten years of chaos many young people today are nihilistic. They only think of themselves . . .'

Zheng noticed Yang frown. In agreement or disagreement?

'How can there be modernization with such attitudes around? Those in charge of our enterprises must tackle the problem. We must learn from experience and find more scientific ways to educate our workers.

'Some people talk as if it's all right to copy the West's science and technology but not its management. I'm not so sure about that. We must study our history, culture and social system too, the working and living conditions of our people.'

Good for him! Although they had been colleagues for so many years, Wang Fangliang could still surprise Zheng.

There had been considerable friction over this meeting. Tian Shoucheng had withdrawn his approval and torn up the speech he had prepared because he suspected that Zheng would come out with some new troublesome proposals. Well, at least it was on record that he had opposed the meeting.

Wang Fangliang had not taken sides, instead he simply held forth on their fine tradition of ideological work which had enabled the revolution to triumph. Later he and Zheng had drawn up an agenda. And as Zheng was still on sick leave Wang had agreed to preside.

Next Zheng spoke about the new problems in economic construction. Material incentives were not enough, he said. Political work was of paramount importance. The ultra-Leftist line had undermined the Party's fine old traditions. They now needed to make a scientific study of how to bring the workers' initiative into play. This involved studying industrial management in other countries, psychology, sociology and behaviourism to meet China's present needs.

Zheng saw a sour look on Wu Guodong's face. Chen Yongming was listening intently. Yang Xiaodong had brightened up.

'There have been changes in industrial management in capitalist countries since the Second World War,' he went on. 'They've come to see that production is affected not just by material conditions but by the workers' state of mind, which is influenced by their home life and relations with others. They've evolved the science of "behaviourism" to arouse enthusiasm and initiative. As it happens, some of our comrades are paying attention to this sort of thing. For instance, Yang Xiaodong, a team leader in the Dawn Motor Works, has solved a lot of problems for his team in this way.' He indicated Yang. 'That's Yang Xiaodong. He's thirty-one.'

Yang fidgeted, his head down, then looked up and met Zheng's eyes.

'Yes, we must try out new methods and sum up our experiences,' agreed Wang. 'Those in charge mustn't be afraid of losing their jobs. We must have more democracy. If you do your work well you'll be re-elected.

'Of course all this will be very complicated, but our socialist enterprises depend on it. You can't treat the masses as fools and then expect them to show initiative.

'Vice-minister Zheng has made a study of personnel management. Shall we ask him to explain his views?'

Applause burst out.

Zheng's heart was playing up again. His left arm felt numb. He noticed that Autumn's face had lit up, making her if not beautiful at least less ugly. Yuanyuan had lost her usual look of flippant wilfulness. And Chen Yongming's expression was rapt but solemn.

'I haven't made a systematic study. I'm only offering you my views for discussion.

'Behaviourism is not a fully developed science. We need

to improve on it on the basis of our own experience, as the Japanese industrialists have done. They've cut down on lost work days by showing concern for their workers, by treating them as more important than machines, and by paying great attention to human relations. That's why their workers show such drive. Of course their behaviourism serves the bosses. But we can use what's scientific about it in our modernization.

'Some comrades think that using foreign methods can only lead to trouble. They're prejudiced. Lenin regarded psychology as one of the cornerstones of dialectical materialism. And our own old philosophers Sun Zi, Mencius and Xun Zi attached immense importance to the study of psychology and human relations. So this isn't something idealistic or foreign.'

What was Zheng Ziyun driving at? Wu Guodong felt completely befogged. But a vice-minister had to be taken seriously. Would he, Wu Guodong, have to change his tried and tested routine? And would what Zheng was proposing work? Wu doubted it. He looked round. When speeches were made in their plant, or during political study, he was used to seeing people sleeping, knitting, whispering or reading the paper. But all were listening intently. Whether they approved or not was another matter.

Zheng noticed some people looking round. Perhaps he was being too abstract for some of these administrators. He changed his tune. 'Now I'll say something about making our political work more scientific.

'First we must have democratic management. Only then can we bring our workers' initiative into play. They must have real power. Why are our trade unions so ineffective? Because under the Party committee the manager has all the power. So the workers aren't their own masters. The Central Committee has now told us to change this. The trade unions are to discuss and decide on major questions. They've the right to propose the dismissal of incompetent administrators. And we're going to have management committees which are not Party committees, made up of experienced, reliable people. A most important decision. But one that won't be easy to carry out.

'That poses a number of questions requiring study . . .' He went on to describe the experience of West Germany and other countries in modernizing industrial management.

Yuanyuan had never heard her father deliver a speech, had no idea how significant his work was. She'd thought all he did was to attend futile meetings. At home he often behaved like an irascible old high official, so that Bamboo made scenes. Now he was showing her his true self. She stole a glance at Autumn, and saw that her small, rather puffy eyes were shining.

Autumn turned to her and said, 'You've such a fine father, you should really love him.' She evidently realized that neither at home nor in the ministry did Zheng find much understanding or support.

Seeing a question in Yuanyuan's eyes she added, 'A man like him belongs not just to his family but to the country.'

Did other people think so highly of dad?

Dozens of tape-recorders were recording his speech.

Chen Yongming was craning forward. In spite of his grizzled hair he appeared capable of fifteen more years of hard work.

Yang Xiaodong was listening raptly, head on one side, lips parted.

An elderly man, a professorial figure, seemed to be following a student's defence of his dissertation. From time to time he frowned, as if dissatisfied with certain formulations.

As for Wu Guodong, he looked like an austere Buddhist suddenly catapulted into the decadence of the Folies Bergères. He was staring about him distractedly as if longing to escape.

Yuanyuan listened more intently as her father went on to expound behaviourist theories about human nature.

'. . . In personnel management, we must respect people, trust them and show concern for them. We can't go on in the ultra-Left way, always looking for new manifestations of class struggle, making everyone live in fear and trembling, afraid to take any initiative . . . A few days ago an old engineer came to see me. Said where he works they don't talk about "stinking intellectuals" any more, but the men in charge still treat them as if they stank. Why have so many overseas Chinese who came back to work here left again? Not because of low living standards, it's because they're not trusted, not rationally used . . .

'If we're to educate people and change how they think and act, we must first improve their living conditions and meet their needs. It's the only way we can bring their initiative into play.

'We must let every individual see their contribution to society and the significance of their work. At the same time we must have targets, supervision and co-ordination. Political work must be adapted to actual conditions, to the level of the people concerned . . .

'Then there's the question of social relationships.

'We talk of unity and stability because unity is a collective's source of strength. An atmosphere of unity and mutual trust makes every group better able to do its job and overcome problems.

'One person can belong to several groups: the Youth League, a welders' team, a football team. There are also anti-social ones such as gangs of young criminals or cliques pursuing selfish interests.

'Some groups don't function properly because they're so badly run that everyone's at odds. Then people either leave or slack. Those are failed groups. As members of society we all want to belong somewhere. If we can't belong to a reputable group, we may join a gang.

'Our industrial managers must give their workers a sense of belonging.

'A successful group must praise its members' achievements and give them public recognition. It must take their proposals seriously and help them when they are in trouble. If they do wrong, it must explain matters to them, not simply ignore them . . .'

Zheng went on to speak of what he had learned from Yang Xiaodong's team (without naming it), about motivation, the art of leadership and about the importance of scientifically trained managers.

'Our enterprises are to have more autonomy and be responsible for their profits or losses. Apart from having ability and political integrity, our managers will have to be in their prime, professionally competent, able to use computers and modern scientific methods . . .'

Chen Yongming felt qualms – could he measure up to this?

'And we must measure the effectiveness of political work scientifically. For some years we studied Chairman Mao's works regardless of the practical results. We competed to see who could write the most copious notes or parrot the most quotations. The effectiveness of political work should be judged by the new wealth created . . .

'We must run our economy according to economic laws and give up our old egalitarian way of all eating from one big pot. That stifles initiative.

'Our universities have an important part to play in making our political work scientific, and they're beginning to co-operate with industry. The president of H— University is an expert of industrial psychology. Next year he's starting a course on it. Although over seventy, he's taking his assistants and research students to make investigations in factories. Some years ago psychology was written off. Now it's making a come-back. Educational psychology's being taught in teachers' training courses. But H— University is the only one tackling industrial psychology. Their president studied it in England. I've written asking the Ministry of Education to allocate him more funds.

'We shall need a liaison office. And a Behaviourism Research Institute, even if it has only fifty people. We'll ask our secretaries in different enterprises to study there. They should be pleased to be able to do some academic research.'

Laughter broke out.

Wang Fangliang laughed too. He thought Zheng too idealistic to be a minister.

There had to be reforms, Wang believed, but Zheng was going the wrong way about this. Foreign methods never worked in China. Zheng didn't understand China. Ever since the Han dynasty the Chinese had taken agriculture more seriously than commerce. Everyone had a small-peasant mentality.

In the ministry Wang was regarded as Zheng's supporter. But why should anyone so smart support a pedant like Zheng? What Wang admired about him was not his rank but his integrity.

Zheng had talked for four hours without a break. His face was flushed and he felt completely limp, his heart beating erratically.

He closed his eyes, slumped against the back of his seat. His car was where he felt most at home. He could relax here, retire into his shell.

His driver Old Yang understood him. He never appeared unduly solicitous, never annoyed Zheng by keeping tabs on him, never discussed his affairs with anyone else.

The street lights came on, stretching away like a scintillating river. The red rear lights of cars flashed past. This was one of the sights of the city.

Zheng wound down the window, letting in the breeze to ruffle his hair. He felt as if sailing towards some unreachable goal.

Would this speech he had just made, like previous ones, vanish without a trace like a snowflake in the desert? The thought depressed him.

Perhaps there was no call to be pessimistic. In Beijing, Shanghai, Harbin and other cities, some enterprises were trying out new methods of industrial management. Life was moving ahead, people were freeing themselves from ignorance and superstition. Their successors would surely be more scientific.

11

There has been a tendency in recent years to attribute all social evils — robbery, rising prices, the housing shortage — to contemporary writing.

After the publication of their report on Chen Yongming, Autumn and Ho Jiabin came under fire, and Zheng was also involved for backing its publication, thus flouting the Party branch's decision not to commend Chen.

Zheng's behaviour baffled others. He broke no laws but kept breaking unwritten rules. Tian was therefore pleased by this development. Give him enough rope and he'd hang himself.

Feng and Commissioner Song, who had also once headed the Dawn Motor Works, came to see Tian. 'Is this report a reflection on us?' they asked.

'I don't understand what's going on,' Tian answered. 'Our Party branch never approved its publication.'

Why should Chen be praised to the skies? Ho Jiabin drew his pay from the ministry, was Feng's subordinate — why didn't he consider the consequences? Well, Feng and Song wouldn't take this lying down.

Tian's secretary Lin told him, 'I hear that Commissioner Song has asked someone to examine Ho Jiabin's dossier.' The 'someone' was Song's wife, a section chief in the personnel department.

'He shouldn't be so blatant about it,' Tian objected. 'Everyone's fed up with this business of checking dossiers.'

'Vice-minister Zheng is said to have been seen strolling with that woman reporter.'

Tian lowered his eyes as if annoyed. 'So what? It's not as if they were caught in bed together!' He knew that Zheng would never have an affair. Only wished he would, for there was nothing more damaging to a man's reputation. In this respect Confucius was truly great. His feudal precepts still held sway in China after more than two millennia. He told Lin, 'Well, you may as well collect reactions to that article for future discussion in our Party branch.' He didn't have to specify what kind of reactions he wanted: Lin could be trusted to make the right selection.

The forum on political work had made Tian eager for a show-down with Zheng.

Zheng's speech had been reported in all the papers. And when the State Council had recently called a meeting to discuss heavy industry someone higher up had added Zheng's name to Tian's list of participants. That made it look as if Tian had discriminated against him.

At the meeting Tian had sat as usual in the front row. The chairman from the State Council had called out, 'Is Zheng Ziyun here?'

What had it meant? Was it a sign of respect?

Zheng had simply answered, 'Present.' For him everything had been plain sailing. In the time of the Gang of Four, not being top man in the ministry, he hadn't had to keep proving his loyalty. He'd spent the campaign against Deng Xiaoping in hospital – out of harm's way. This same higher-up had smiled quizzically at Tian.

'Comrade Shoucheng, everyone else is in hospital. You're the only one still fit.'

Tian had something else preying on his mind. When Jiang Qing* had come to see an industrial exhibition he had ordered one of their factories to make her a stainless steel chamberpot as a token of his regard. No one had yet mentioned it, but it couldn't have been forgotten. He'd never live that chamberpot down.

The State Council man, who had asked Zheng to sit in front, had told him appreciatively, 'Your ministry has been doing very well.'

This indicated that Zheng might soon be promoted and take Tian's place. Of course, in China an ex-minister could never be downgraded to washing dishes. So long as he

---

* The widow of Mao Zedong and a member of the disgraced Gang of Four.

104

committed no serious political mistake – and he was extremely careful – he ought to keep his ministerial rank for life.

But Zheng constituted a menace. Though he wouldn't stoop to playing dirty tricks, he knew all that went on behind the scenes and might spill the beans one day. If his impractical reformist ideas really won approval higher up there would be the devil to pay.

The dispute over that article had not been a real trial of strength. The time for that had not come. Tian must sit tight till someone intervened to halt this new trend. To fight his battle for him.

All these years, he believed, he had shown himself a true dialectical materialist.

The Party branch meeting was nearing its conclusion. Tian looked at his watch: 11.30. Just enough time to bring up the questions of Ho Jiabin's report. No need to say too much, just start the ball rolling.

'We've half an hour left,' he said. 'There's another question. The last couple of years some writers have talked a lot about intervening in life. Now a writer's written a report about Comrade Chen Yongming of the Dawn Motor Works – intervening in our ministry! So it seems we have talents here too!' He laughed.

He knew that if someone were to write a novel about his own ministry, there would be the devil to pay. Those in the know would be able to identify every character in it. And the novel would be sold all over the country, might even be recommended to some vice-premier . . .

Tian continued, 'I'm a rough and ready fellow. Don't understand literature. But in Yan'an in the old days Chairman Mao taught us that literature and art should serve the workers, peasants and soldiers, serve proletarian politics. Well . . .'

Wang Fangliang interjected with a laugh, 'Haven't you read the papers recently?'

Unnerved by Wang's laughter Tian went straight to the point. 'Our Party branch didn't approve of publishing that report. But Comrade Ziyun insisted it should be published, and later it caused a lot of talk. Perhaps Comrade Ziyun didn't understand our objections as he was away on sick leave.'

'I did,' put in Zheng. 'But go on.'

'The main objections were: 1. That report isn't true to the facts; 2. Chen Yongming attacks others to boost himself; 3. He takes the credit for other people's work; 4. Politically he's unreliable. In a word, the social effect of that report is to undermine unity and stability.'

Commissioner Song chimed in, 'He couldn't have raised production in the time of the Gang of Four. I could have done just as well now. I didn't make a go of it because I followed Party principles.'

People can always justify their actions.

Many of those present accepted Song's code of conduct.

At any period in history those who have the courage of their convictions are a minority.

Vice-minister Kong Xiang boomed, 'It all boils down to collective leadership. Any successes should be attributed to the Party Committee. It's wrong to single out any individual.'

Kong was fuming. What the hell did writers understand about politics? Why shove their oar in? There ought to be another anti-Rightist campaign to pack them off to labour camps. If that didn't shut them up, then shoot a couple. Men like him had liberated China and had the wounds to prove it, yet here were these scribblers laying down the law. Ridiculous! Point a gun at them and they'd shit themselves.

In the month since Zheng's speech about political work his intellectual mannerisms had infuriated Kong.

Zheng's speech had stuck in his gullet. He couldn't pinpoint what was wrong with it, could hardly understand it. Instinctively, though, he felt it a threat to him.

It wouldn't pay to oppose Zheng openly, as Zheng outranked him; and in any case Kong had no idea how to refute him.

Good! Tian felt that Kong had hit the nail on the head, and that his target was Zheng. But nobody followed up. They had all grown too cautious to risk offending colleagues.

All that could be heard was the hum of the electric fan.

Someone had turned the fan full on. Zheng, sitting right in front of it, stood up and moved to an armchair by the door, where he had a view of the poplars outside and the blue sky.

He ought to go out to the countryside some Sunday. Before the Cultural Revolution he had taken Yuanyuan hunting. His rifle, confiscated when his place was raided, had been returned to him. But like him it was old and rusty.

Zheng's inscrutable expression provoked Song Ke – you never knew what the fellow was really thinking.

This meeting exasperated Commissioner Song. The others all refused to speak out, but he could hardly say any more himself, being personally involved.

He was jealous of Chen Yongming. It was owing to Chen that his name had been removed from the list of candidates for vice-ministerships. And Zheng had boosted Chen, made him manager of the Dawn Works as if to show up Song's incompetence.

He longed to see them both worsted. Opposed them on every issue. He had come to this meeting hoping that his colleagues would denounce them. But he had been disappointed. Zheng looked unruffled.

Song angrily stubbed out his cigarette, then sloshed tea into the ashtray.

At this point Kong Xiang said, 'I've heard that the woman journalist who helped Ho Jiabin write that report has been divorced twice!' He darted a warning glance at Zheng. To him divorcees ranked with prostitutes.

The meeting livened up: all heads turned towards Kong.

The Marriage Law allowed divorce if husband and wife were incompatible, Zheng was thinking, so why did a lecher like Kong regard it as a crime?

Wang Fangliang straightened up in his armchair and said loudly, 'This is a Party meeting.' He would have spoken more harshly, but didn't want to offend Kong over this issue. Kong was in charge of personnel. When Wang had tried to get the daughter of an old comrade-in-arms transferred to the ministry, Kong had not only turned her down but reported him for this infringement of discipline, and Wang had been given a lecture. The hypocrites! He had cursed Kong to his subordinates, listing the jobs he had found for relatives, his carryings-on with women. Since then the two men had not been on speaking terms.

Now Wang said, 'The writers of that article told me Chen Yongming hadn't read it before its publication. He didn't know the contents. I rang up Chen too and asked him if he'd read it. He said he hadn't.

'I told him it had caused a big commotion in the ministry and asked him his view on that.

'He said, "In China you can only write up dead people, not living ones."

'I thoroughly agree. China's overpopulated, with not enough for everyone to do. A single report can turn our whole ministry upside down and has to be discussed by our Party branch. Have we nothing better to do with our time? One municipal committee held three meetings to discuss whether women could perm their hair . . . We can't cope with big problems and waste our time over piddling things like this.'

This made Tian feel uneasy. Even the biggest nincompoop there would see that he should have raised these objections himself.

At once he backed down. 'Apparently the article isn't factual enough, but that's not Chen's responsibility.'

The faces of Kong Xiang and Song Ke clouded over.

Zheng asked, 'Do you blame the writers? That's no way to look at the problem. Let's check up on the so-called factual errors. I'll have that done before we reach a conclusion. We must also find out whether the Party branch opposed its publication. In the first place, as far as I know, I wasn't the only one absent from that day's meeting.' He looked at Tian and went on, 'Secondly, when you had your discussion, quite a few of the branch hadn't read the article. Thirdly, only a minority expressed opposition to it.' He stopped to puff at his cigarette, then added with a smile,

'We seem to have set ourselves up as literary critics. If I didn't have my own work, I'd write a novel. As it is, I mean to write a favourable review of the article. Comrade Tian Shoucheng spoke of its social effects. I agree with his approach. But how do we judge them? Do we listen to officials or to ordinary readers? Consider the short-term or the long-term effects?

'I think the report's had a good social effect. I know some young workers in that plant. One of them came round to see me, bringing that magazine. Costs one yuan twenty cents. I asked him, "Why spend 3.5 per cent of your pay on this?" He's a grade-two worker.

'He said, "It's great!"

'I asked, "How?"

'"Well," he said, "it's about our factory manager. You'd know if you read it."

'I said, "It's bound to be exaggerated."

'He said, "No, it's all true, but it didn't go far enough. If you don't believe me, go and ask my mates."

'Know how I felt? I envied Chen Yongming. I only wish my subordinates felt like that about me.

'Of course, some people disapprove of Chen because he disbanded the Daqing office and the political section . . .

'We've no right to pour cold water on managers like Chen. If we do we're discouraging thousands of workers. China has too few such cadres. We ought to protect him. I'm not saying he has no faults. He's too strict, sometimes hurts people's feelings, isn't democratic enough. But nobody is perfect, no article either. We can fault the article for not giving a more accurate picture of Chen Yongming, but we should give the writers credit for having the courage to describe a new kind of hero.'

Tian decided to let the matter drop, to recoup this loss some other way. He adjourned the meeting.

Zheng woke up from his siesta feeling limp, with a bitter taste in his mouth. He got up, brewed a cup of tea, then stood by the window overlooking the street.

Some youngsters just back from swimming had colourful trunks hanging from their handlebars, waving in the wind like flags. The girl on the carrier of one bike looked like Yuanyuan. Her arms folded, her long bronze legs outstretched, she didn't seem afraid of falling off.

Yuanyuan had recently quarrelled with Bamboo again. They were always having rows in their family. Talk of stability and unity! She was getting a sharp tongue, like him. She had said rudely to Bamboo, 'Want to take me to the horse-market again? You ought to be running a stud-farm.'

Heavens, what a girl!

She refused to discuss marriage with her parents. 'Everyone has secrets,' she said. 'You have yours too.'

Zheng only wished he had.

There were trees outside and passers-by. In the hot sunshine everyone seemed rather listless. Only the old woman with a shrivelled, nut-brown face selling ice-lollies was loudly hawking her wares. She was about his own age, but far more vigorous. He felt he already had one foot in the grave. A secretary, maidservant, office and chauffeur-driven car had made him soft.

He was in a foul temper. Why? Because he was lonely?

The telephone in next room rang. Good – a diversion.

When Bamboo took the call, he knew from her dry, supercilious tone that she was talking to someone she disliked and he liked.

'It's for you, Zheng,' she said. 'That woman Ye again.'

Her voice was so loud that Autumn must have heard it.

'Yes, Zheng Ziyun here.'

Autumn sounded rather overwrought. 'The editorial board has forwarded an anonymous letter to me!'

'What does it say?' Zheng noticed that Bamboo had pricked up her ears, stopped fanning herself.

'That they shouldn't have published my article. I'm a tramp, I've been sleeping with the man who helped me write it, as well as the man we wrote up. And I'm chasing a certain vice-minister – Your Excellency.'

110

'I'm very sorry about this.' Zheng felt as apologetic as if he had insulted her.

'Strange, isn't it? But nothing new.'

'Is there anything I can do for you?'

Bamboo flung her folding fan on to the table. Zheng tightened his hold on the receiver to prevent her from grabbing it.

'No, thanks. I only told you to put you on your guard. Goodbye!'

'Goodbye.'

This was really the limit.

Zheng's talk on political work had impressed many theoreticians and administrators. People flocked to the ministry to ask for copies of it and accounts of the research work being done. They were received by the office research team which had supplied Zheng with much of his material.

Then, all of a sudden, Tian announced that such requests should be handled by his secretary.

What that meant was very clear.

Now they were smearing a woman powerless to defend herself. Too cowardly to tackle real abuses, they struck hard when it came to attacking a woman.

Bamboo flared up at him. 'You're sorry? What for? What d'you want to do for her?'

Zheng glared at her. In her elegant silk dressing-gown embroidered with a pair of phoenixes, her hair dyed black and permed, she seemed completely out of place in his casually furnished room.

They had been married now for forty years. But he felt increasingly estranged from her.

'Why not go and see a doctor?' he suggested.

'Don't talk to me that way!' She hit the arm of the sofa with her fan.

'You're so morbidly suspicious of all other women. Have you no self-respect? I can't understand women like you. On International Women's Day you shout about the emancipation of women. But at home you depend on your husbands like feudal wives. Political and economic equality

isn't enough. Women have got to emancipate themselves.'
He stopped, eyeing her hair and clothes. 'You should get
ahead, win your husbands' respect. Not just doll yourselves
up . . .' He wanted to say that common interests and
understanding should be the basis of love. But if he said this
she might suspect that he wanted to divorce her.

Bamboo's anger and jealousy gave way to fear. What was
Zheng up to? Why lecture her on how women should retain
their husbands' love?

She knew he no longer had any feeling for her.

She started sobbing. A woman's tears are more potent
that reasoning. Zheng said no more.

Someone knocked at the door. It was half-past three,
time for his secretary to deliver papers and documents.
With a sense of relief Zheng went to open the door.
Bamboo stopped sobbing and padded back to her room. At
least she never made him lose face in public.

Zheng's secretary Ji should have been in the KGB. Sensing
the strained atmosphere, his eyes swept the room. There
were no teacups on the table, evidently no one had called.
Everything was in its right place – but something was
wrong. He waited while Zheng leafed through the documents.

Finally, putting them down, Zheng asked, 'Has the
ministry chosen the team to inspect the Dawn Motor
Works?'

'Yes.' Ji never wasted words. He liked to keep Zheng
guessing.

'Who's in charge?'

'Section Chief Zhu Yiping.'

Not even a commissioner! This must be Song Ke's doing.

'Anyone from the Enterprise Management Department?'

'No.'

This was unprecedented.

Did Tian Shoucheng know? Even if he did he would
sham deaf and dumb.

'Anything else?' asked Ji.

112

'No, thanks.'

Zheng was tempted to head this inspection team himself. But he couldn't have his own way in everything.

Chen Yongming, burly Chen Yongming, was going to feel isolated again.

There were still Yang Xiaodong and his mates. He shouldn't lose hope.

What would the ordinary workers think? They were bound to feel shabbily treated.

Zheng Ziyun, although a vice-minister, was helpless. In the same predicament as Chen Yongming.

He sighed and shook his head. Then sat down at his desk and picked up a sheet of paper.

> Comrade Chen Yongming:
>   Your reorganization of the Dawn Motor Works in the last year has been outstanding. My poor health won't permit me to join in the coming check-up. I hope it goes well.
>   Greetings!
>   Zheng Ziyun

Poor health? The usual pretext for stalling.

12

Autumn's hand was trembling as she paid for her telephone call.

'Why did you have to say all that over the phone?' protested Ho Jiabin as they came out of the Telephone Building.

'What else could I do? Trouble him in the ministry and cause a lot more talk? If I call on him at home, his wife is too overbearing.'

'You didn't have to tell him.'

'He ought to know. To be on his guard.' She sighed.

'You sorry?' he asked.

'No, upset.'

'What does it matter? We did what we could. So why shouldn't we pay the price?'

'But the price is too high!'

'You take your reputation so seriously?'

'Don't you?'

'No, if people gun for you, what can you do? Drop dead? Don't let them get you down. A good name, like possessions, is something extraneous.'

'In that case why do you want to join the Party?' She smiled as if she had checkmated him.

'Not for the sake of my reputation, but because I believe in Marxism. Want to study and practise it, to help reform the Party. Too many members still have a small peasant mentality instead of being scientific Marxists.'

Autumn looked round vigilantly. He was crazy! If she hadn't known Ho since their college days she would have thought him mentally deranged. 'Keep your voice down!' she scolded.

'Why should I? That's not counter-revolutionary talk!' He had raised his voice.

She put up one hand to stop him. 'If you talk that way you'll land yourself in trouble.' She glared at him. 'I'm surprised your Party branch passed you.'

He had wanted to stop her worrying, but instead had added to her anxiety.

In the twenty years and more since they left college, they had found endless subjects to dispute. He invariably ended up by backing down.

He confronted Autumn now and threw out his hands. 'In what way am I unfit to be a Party member? Have I less sense of social responsibility than Feng Xiaoxian and Grace? All right, Autumn, I know what worries you. I'll look out.'

She smiled in self-derision. 'I'm teaching you to be foxy.'

'Can't be done! Of course you're a realist. If not for Commissioner Fang they wouldn't have passed me. It wasn't Grace who got me in. She spread all kinds of rumours . . . Goes without saying she has plenty against me. I talk too carelessly.'

'In what way?'

'I approve of the weakening of the family in bourgeois society. Well, why not? When there's an end to private ownership, the family will have to be broken up. By then people's lives won't be restricted by laws . . . So they accuse me of preaching promiscuity! The idiots. All these years after Liberation we pay attention only to the theory of class struggle – which we've distorted – not to Marxist aesthetics, ethics or views on love and marriage.'

'You're talking about centuries to come.' Autumn smiled. 'What does it matter if they can't grasp those today? You should make allowances for their mental level.'

'Then Grace criticized my stand. She said, "You want everyone's pay to go up by five grades, and say the state owes it to the people. What stand are you taking?"

'I told her, "I don't remember saying five grades, but I do believe everyone should have a rise."

'She demanded, "Don't you know the country's hard up?"

'I said, "Could have been avoided. We should be clear about the reasons for our present difficulties. I don't believe you've really thought about them."

'"Me?!" She'd pinned a label on me, not expecting me to throw it back at her. Raising her eyebrows she fumed, "What can I do? I'm not the premier."

'"It's very simple. Introduce more rational promotion. Someone like Luo should never have got a rise. Nobody proposed him, but you insisted. Everyone wanted Wen to get one, but you crossed his name off. So everyone complained. You transferred their resentment against you to the system, wasn't that increasing the state's difficulties?"

'She pounded the desk and snapped, "What we're considering now is whether or not you're fit to join the Party."

'I said, "I'll make a note of this. Thumping the desk and trying to intimidate me. Who do you think you are? I'm not your servant, I'm a state functionary."

'So then she reported me to Feng Xiaoxian. He reprimanded me, because even if she was in the wrong she was my superior and represented the Party.

'Why equate those in authority with the Party?

'Last of all they found fault with my lifestyle. Because I'm concerned for Joy. It's not easy for a widow. . .'

'Ah, she ought to marry again.' Autumn took an oversimplified view of other people's marriages.

'Marry again? The man she loves won't marry her.'

'You mean Fang Wenxuan?'

In the Cultural Revolution Fang had been removed from his post and expelled from the Party, so his wife had asked for a divorce, turning in his diaries to show she had broken with him. As his diaries queried certain policies, he had been beaten up and had a rib broken. His wife had taken over all their belongings.

In 1970, in the cadre school, Fang was cleared and made head of their brigade. Then Joy's husband committed suicide, leaving her to cope with a new-born child – Ho could never forgive him for his selfishness.

Of course he had been under tremendous pressure.

The cadre school had been set up in a labour-reform camp, where they only had one day off in ten and conditions were hard.

Joy was given a kitchen to live in, a room so low that Ho could hardly stand upright.

It was dark and dank with mildew on the earth floor. Everything turned mouldy in there. In the freezing winter they burned charcoal up in the hills and carried it down on their backs. Incessant rain made the steep paths slippery. With their heavy loads they kept falling and covered themselves with mud.

One morning while it was still dark, a whistle summoned everyone else to fall in. Joy was left all alone with her baby, feeling helpless and apathetic.

She knew she ought to be going with the others to fetch charcoal, but couldn't drag herself up.

The baby's hot-water bottle was cold, it ought to be

refilled. His nappies hanging overhead were wet, and she had none left to change him. She longed for a bowl of hot noodles, though as a small girl she had detested noodles.

Where could she find a brazier to dry the nappies, boil water and make noodles? She never liked asking favours. Especially not now as a 'counter-revolutionary's widow'.

Self-pity wouldn't help matters. Weak as she was, she had to bring up her little son.

What Joy felt was not so much mother love as increased responsibility. She took the hardships of her confinement for granted. Just hoped the time would pass quickly, till this was no more than a painful memory.

When damp charcoal sputtered in the other cells and people sat round their little earthen stoves chatting, Joy's door, forgotten by everyone else, was opened. In came Fang Wenxuan and Ho Jiabin carrying two sacks of charcoal. Streaked with mud, drenched with rain, they bore no resemblance to a commissioner or the graduate of a well-known university. Yet, cold, hungry and exhausted, they had taken pity on a helpless widow.

Fang's grey hair was sopping wet, his lips blue with cold . . . a wretched sight.

Yet, strangely, the two of them reminded Joy of Father Christmas. Of the fancy-dress balls at her college on New Year's Eve and the presents boys put on the window-ledges of the girls' dorm on Women's Day . . . That had been in fun, however, whereas this had been a reply to a harsh kind of morality.

Fang seemed to have forgotten the cadre school, the suicide of Joy's husband, her counter-revolutionary label. . . He asked casually, 'Where's your charcoal-burner?'

Ho Jiabin pulled it out from under the bed piled with litter.

'Got any kindling?' asked Fang.

Ho rummaged under the bed again. 'No, there isn't any.'

Fang went out. He came back with a fir stump and a chopper. Cut kindling and lit the fire.

He looked at the smoke-blackened ceiling, at the water

trickling under the door, the empty water vat in one corner, the dirty bowls and chopsticks in a bucket, the bottles, mostly empty, one containing a little salt. Fang, a communist, blamed himself for his inhumanity. When her husband committed suicide and she most needed help, why hadn't he come to see her? He had been afraid of losing his newly-recovered freedom.

Before leaving he said, 'If you need anything, let us know. That's not asking favours, it's your right. You owe it to the baby.'

How wonderful to have a fire! Joy felt as if she had come out of a coma.

Ho Jiabin fetched water, washed up and tidied the room.

From time to time he glanced at Joy sitting motionless on her bed, and tried not to disturb her.

He fetched rice from the canteen, put it in her pan, added salt and water, then boiled it on the stove and put in a handful of greens. Indicating a small jar of lard he said, 'Old Fang asked the canteen for this.'

Joy had let them wait on her, not even thanking them. But as she raised the bowl of rice to her lips the tears poured down her cheeks.

After that, when a pig was killed for the canteen she received the trotters and liver; when their driver came back from town there was milk powder for her. Now that someone had given the lead, other people too came knocking on her door.

Ho noticed that Joy eked out the charcoal Fang had taken her. When she had to burn it, she sat basking in its warmth.

Fang's sympathy and concern had won her heart. She was still only a girl.

Ho sensed that her love for him would come to nothing.

She ought to understand the sort of life Fang had lived all these years. He had been moulded by his environment. Even if he loved her he would conform to type. Then she would sink into despair again. Ho was powerless to prevent this.

But it was touching to watch them. Ho saw genuine feeling in Fang's eyes, and Joy was dove-like in her affection.

For a time he thought his misgivings unwarranted, forgot Joy's label and believed they might marry as Fang's wife had left him, although she had never formally divorced him.

This illusion was short-lived, however. On their return to Beijing Fang Wenxuan resumed office and his wife rejoined him.

Fang had a guilty conscience and kept telling himself he had let Joy down.

He felt he had made an irreparable mistake. Grew sterner, more of an introvert, more stand-offish and capricious. Those unaware of his wretchedness thought this the result of his restoration to power.

The whole bureau knew that his feeling for Joy, once legitimate, was now illegitimate. If he so much as glanced at her in the corridor there was talk. Most people sympathized, others were hoping for some dramatic dénouement. How could Fang blame them? Men like Feng Xiaoxian took advantage of this to run him down on the sly to Vice-minister Kong. Sometimes in his frustration he longed to resign and go far, far away. Out of the question of course. He had to go where he was told.

When they had walked as far as Nanchizi, Ho looked at his watch. It was after four. 'Shall I see you home?' he offered.

'No, I'm going back to my office.' Autumn, over her resentment, appeared to have changed back into a robot. 'And you, going back to the ministry?' she asked.

'Not I. With the cuts in capital construction there's nothing for me to do. Three hundred of us are just sitting idle.'

'Can't you find anything to do?'

'When I wrote about Chen Yongming that stirred up a hornet's nest.'

'Why didn't you tell me?'

'Why should I? At the worst, Feng Xiaoxian will keep me out of the Party. They weren't unanimous in the branch about admitting me.'

'That would be terrible.'

'Who cares?'

'Well, see you later.'

Autumn boarded her bus and waved goodbye to Ho, who simply nodded. Through the back window he watched her tall, thin figure swaying as the bus drove towards the setting sun. Where should he go? As Autumn knew, like her he kept occupying himself with other people's business. But neither regretted the time and energy spent.

Ho Jiabin walked into a shop and asked, 'What have you got for someone with dysentery?'

Joy's son, just getting over a bad bout of dysentry, had been discharged from the hospital today.

The shop assistant said drily, 'Furazolidone.'

Ho thanked her, then bought a sponge cake, a bottle of orangeade and a package of glucose.

It wasn't the rush hour yet, but the bus was packed. To his disgust there was a row on it between a surly Beijing youth and a Northeastern woman loaded with luggage who bumped into him. Ho could not help intervening to defend her, but after he did the woman showed she could give as good as she got.

The untidy room reminded Fang Wenxuan of Joy's hut in the cadre school farm. It smelt of the little boy's vomit. The curtain, made out of one of her old skirts, was as faded and worn as its owner. She needed someone to care for her, to organize her life for her. But she had never remarried. Was it because of him? If only she still loved him . . . That was no way to think. He ought to forget her.

The little boy on the bed was staring listlessly out of the window. He had his mother's eyes. Fang remembered cuddling him when he was a baby. He had never held Joy in his arms.

Joy sitting by the bed on a rickety chair, had her hands limply in her lap. They were even thinner now than in the cadre school. Her face showed nothing but exhaustion.

Why had he come to see her? Her son was ill. She was in trouble. But was this a pretext?

'Why didn't you phone to say you were fetching him home from hospital? You could have had my car.' In fact, he wouldn't have offered it if she had phoned for fear the driver might talk.

'There was no need,' said Joy. 'I called a cab.'

'How did you carry him?'

'The driver helped.' She turned to her son. 'What would you like to eat?'

'Pickled gherkins.'

'I'll get them,' offered Fang eagerly. 'What else?'

'Just rice porridge and pickled gherkins.' The boy sounded cross. He wished this visitor would go and leave his mother in peace. 'Boil me some rice porridge, mum,' he begged. 'I'm hungry.'

When Joy looked in the pan there were left-over noodles in it. If they lived together, Fang thought, he could run things for her. But what would people say if he asked for a divorce? They would try to dissuade him, warn him. 'Which matters more to you – politics or love?' In other words, 'Do you want to keep your post?' As if love were something bourgeois, incompatible with revolutionary politics, as reprehensible as smoking opium. All his friends and colleagues would cold-shoulder him.

Fang should have realized that these specious arguments, camouflaged as communist ethics, were in fact a defence of feudal ethics.

But he failed to see this. As Ho Jiabin had often remarked to Joy, 'Those commissioners who drive everywhere by car, as if they were rushed off their feet, rarely see anything clearly.'

Fang, caught in his predicament, envied those who could drink to drown their cares. Would he ever be able to take life easy like that?

Joy sniffed at the left-over noodles, then frowned. 'Rancid!' She went to empty them out.

Fang felt superfluous.

He followed her to the kitchen.

Having scoured the pan she washed the rice with an energy that struck him as excessive.

'Forgive me, Joy.'

'What for?' She kept her back to him. 'You made me no promises so what is there to forgive?'

'Make allowances for me then.'

Of course, allowances have to be made for weak characters.

Something deep in Joy's heart seemed to take wing suddenly – to soar off like a bird.

'Please leave me,' she said.

Fang fumbled in his pocket, stammering, 'I want to leave you some money, I'm sure you can use it.'

'You know I won't take it.'

Of course. He withdrew his hand awkwardly.

'Now go.'

He left.

As he fingered the peeling door frame on his way out he knew he could never come back. This untidy room and its occupants belonged to a different world, and so did everything that had passed between them.

Through the window Joy watched Fang Wenxuan walk to the bus stop. He hadn't come by car.

When she went back her son asked, 'Are you crying, mum?'

'No!' She cleared and wiped the table.

He clenched his puny fists. 'When I'm big, if anyone bullies you I'll punch his head.'

Bless his little heart! By the time he grew up he would understand that certain problems cannot be solved by force.

She raised her head, her eyes closed, and sighed.

Ho Jiabin came in covered in sweat. 'I knocked but no one answered,' he complained. 'So I just marched in, sorry.' He put down his packages. 'Well, is he back to normal?'

Seeing her standing with closed eyes, he lowered his voice. 'What's wrong?'

Joy threw herself into his arms like a child unfairly treated. 'Jiabin, Jiabin!' she sobbed. 'Why is everything so difficult?'

He patted her shoulder. 'Because this is a time of transition, of sudden changes, ups and downs . . . Don't take things too much to heart.' He dried her tears for her. 'No single individual or group is to blame, we're all going through growing-pains.'

The little boy cried, 'Mum!'

Joy brushed her eyes with the back of one hand. She smiled apologetically, rather shyly. 'Look at the goodies uncle has brought you,' she said.

He pushed aside the cake she was holding out. This wasn't what he needed. He needed to grow up quickly, till he was as big as Uncle Ho, able to look after her.

13

Jade worked to a tight schedule.

First thing that morning she switched on the radio and listened to the six o'clock news while making the bed. On her way to the kitchen for the broom, she dumped yesterday's laundry in the tub in the passage. Having lit the gas-stove to steam buns, she swept the floor, and wiped the table. And while the soybean milk was heating she washed her face and brushed her teeth.

By half-past six her older boy Qiang had his younger brother Zhuang dressed and washed.

As today was a Monday she had to take Zhuang to the kindergarten where he was a weekly boarder. When only his brother was at home they didn't have to get up till 6.25.

Still, life was less of a rush now than before.

After Wu Guodong was taken into hospital, Chen Yongming had arranged her a transfer to a hairdresser's nearer home, so that she didn't have to waste time on the bus and saved three yuan fifty on her monthly ticket too. He had helped her find a new kindergarten for the younger boy as well.

Apart from Wu's hepatitis, things were going fine for them. Life was easier than with him at home.

Yesterday Yang Xiaodong and Wu Bin had changed her gas cylinder for her when they delivered her husband's pay packet. Yang had pounded up to the fifth floor, the cylinder on his back, without even panting.

They had bought her rice, cornmeal and flour from the grain shop.

Yang urged her, 'If something needs doing, just say the word. Don't hesitate.'

Jade remembered her husband complaining, 'Those young fellows in our workshop don't take anything seriously. They just fool about.'

She could see nothing wrong with these lively youngsters. Wu Bin had amused the boys by standing on his head, then lifted the younger one and whirled him around while she watched nervously.

Her sons had whooped with laughter.

With their father they couldn't let themselves go like that. They had to keep a wary eye on him, and even Jade felt constrained. When she and Wu first went out, they had sat on a bench in Beihai Park and studied the Party Constitution for two hours. Young people nowadays would hardly believe it. Each time they met they discussed their political study and the progress they'd made before going to look at the goldfish or row a boat. Young people nowadays walked arm in arm or even kissed in public.

Her husband neither smoked nor drank. Each month he made over all his pay to her. He didn't laze about, leaving her all the housework. Nor did he insist on scrambled eggs and two ounces of liquor for supper while she and the children ate cornmeal muffins and cheap pickles. He wasn't a bad man. What exhausted her was the way he kept nagging.

When she had rolled up her sleeves to make dumplings for these two youngsters they had stopped her laughingly. 'Old Wu's told us what good dumplings you make,' Yang had said, 'but we've important business today. It won't wait.'

'What?'

'I'm helping him find a girlfriend,' Yang had pretended to whisper in her ear.

With that they had hurried away.

Only later did she realize that they hadn't wanted her to spend money on them. She couldn't understand what Wu Guodong found objectionable about them.

Jade walked ahead, carrying a small quilt and mattress. It was turning cold, and Zhuang needed warmer bedding at the kindergarten. She glanced at her watch. Must hurry or she'd be late. When she looked round the small boy was fumbling with his shoelaces – he couldn't tie them. With a sigh she went back, put her bundle on the ground and did them for him. No use scolding: he was so small, and he hadn't cried or sulked when woken up – he was a good boy.

Just then Mo Zheng rode past on his bike. 'Give me that bundle. I'll give you both a lift to the kindergarten.'

Jade felt surprised, also a little embarrassed. When Wu was at home Mo Zheng steered clear of them. Her husband treated him as if he might rob them. Called him 'a stone in a latrine, hard and stinking'. He had a low opinion of Autumn too. A middle-aged spinster adopting a thief – the idea!

Now this hard, stinking stone was helping them.

'I don't want to make you late for work.'

'I can ride faster and make up the time.'

Mo Zheng put her bundle on the carrier.

Wu Guodong let out a yell, waking all the patients from their midday nap.

'What's up, Old Wu?' someone asked.

'Nothing, sorry. I had a nightmare.'

'What did you dream about?' the youngster in the next bed asked.

How could he tell him?

This youngster, whose job was repairing umbrellas, spent all his time planning a novel. In Wu's month or more in hospital, his manuscript had grown as thick as a brick. He noted down jokes that were made, news from the different places where people worked, and complaints and gripes.

When the youngster went to the toilet Wu had rummaged through the books by his bed. Plekhanov's *On Art*. In the Party school he'd learned that Plekhanov had opposed Lenin and was a revisionist. Why read him instead of Chairman Mao?

A book on sculpture had photographs of nude figures on its cover. Wu dropped it, flushing, looking round to see if anyone else had noticed. Luckily no one had.

The youngster's crew-cut reminded him of Yang Xiaodong. He must be another awkward customer.

Wu fished the towel out from the cupboard by his bed and mopped his perspiring face, then turned over to avoid the sarcastic eyes of his young neighbour.

It had been a strange dream.

He had dreamed that Yang Xiaodong and those other young devils had climbed on to the overhead travelling crane to shit. Then the workshop had turned into an ice-rink, where they had skated around, turning out first-rate parts. Everything had whirled about, making Wu dizzy. The public-address system had announced at full blast, 'That will be followed by a ventriloquist act.'

Barking and caterwauling . . .

'Cut off the power!' Wu had bellowed.

But no one had paid any attention. 'You're not in charge here any more,' they had jeered.

He had stamped on the ice, fallen flat on his face, and woken up with a start.

How could he tell this dream to anyone?

Wu sighed. His eye fell on the chair by the window where Yang Xiaodong had sat that morning.

Yang was head of the workshop now. A lightning promotion! He couldn't even sit still. Chen Yongming had put him in charge of their political study too.

And not even a Party member!

'What's new in the plant?' Wu had asked him.

'We had a dance on National Day!' Yang had told him provocatively.

'A dance? Who organized it?'

'The Youth League.'

'Did the Party Committee approve?'

'It was Manager Chen's idea.'

Weren't things lively enough already? Dark glasses, bell-bottomed trousers, cassettes, and now dancing! Surely someone must have protested.

'What was the general reaction?'

'It was great. Even the manager danced. And the technicians were great, much better than us. They had style. You should have seen Old Chen waltzing with his wife. He told us to spruce up, to scent ourselves, and to bow to a girl before asking her for a dance. Said this was a good chance to find ourselves girlfriends! Quite right too. Much better than with go-betweens.'

The other patients were all ears. Some chuckled, some tutted.

One of them, a professor, commented, 'Dancing is a civilized recreation. I don't know why people say it produces hooligans. That's nonsense. Young people only become hooligans when they've no proper outlet for their energy . . .'

Trust an intellectual to approve of these bourgeois tastes. He was always listening to sentimental music.

The young umbrella repairer said, 'Hear, hear!'

The fleshy butcher opposite growled, 'I don't believe it. All I know is that people feel terrible if they get no meat for three days.'

Another elderly man, a civil servant, remarked, 'Your

manager sounds as though he's going a bit too far. Don't you read the papers? There's a new trend this year: they're publishing readers' letters against dancing. Some places are still holding dances on the quiet. But they'll soon be out.'

Wu Guodong was really worried that Chen Yongming might slip up. But he admired Chen's drive and could make allowances for him.

'How's everything in the workshop?' he asked.

'OK,' said Yang.

Wu knew it was no use fretting. Besides, he was too sleepy to keep his eyes open. After Yang left he had dozed off and had another nightmare.

Inspecting the wards that morning Radiance had discovered that Wu Guodong had no appetite. So she'd rung up Jade to ask her to bring one of his favourite dishes. She wondered if she'd done Jade a good turn or a bad one.

'I asked Old Wu what he'd like to eat, but he wouldn't say. I could cook him something, but I'm sure he prefers your cooking.'

She knew that Jade was busy. With a full-time job and two children, she must be worn out.

Jade thanked her for her thoughtfulness.

Now the telephone rang again.

'Hullo, who do you want?'

'I'm coming to pick you up this evening, Radiance.' Chen Yongming must be using a public telephone. He had raised his voice because of the din around.

'To pick me up?' Radiance was surprised. 'Where are you?'

'In town.'

'Why?' He had only returned from the provinces yesterday and should have been taking the day off.

'I'll tell you when I see you. Just wait for me.'

When she came off duty Radiance smoothed her hair and went out to look for her husband's jeep. She sat down on a bench by the gate to wait.

An orderly was sweeping the yard.

Radiance loved her hospital. This old, weather-stained building was home to her. Here she had met Chen Yong-ming, had her two babies.

It was in the back of nowhere. The patients who came here were not driven in cars or escorted by secretaries. Some of them wore homespun, smoked home-grown tobacco. They were honest, hard working folk, the salt of the earth.

And she was one of them. Not specially talented, her name would not appear in the annals of medicine and she would never be invited to lecture. But she was a thoroughly conscientious doctor, devoted to her patients.

A quarter past seven. Why wasn't he here? Radiance grew rather uneasy. Normally he was punctual and never wasted time. He never let his colleagues talk for more than ten minutes at meetings in the plant.

Could he have had an accident? He drove too fast.

From time to time she went to the gate to look for his jeep – in vain.

She sat disconsolately on the bench, close to tears.

It grew dark. When a Red Flag limousine drove in, she paid no attention, not even wondering why someone in such a superior car should come to their hospital.

Then Chen was standing before her. 'Were you anxious?'

Relieved yet resentful she scolded, 'I was afraid you'd had an accident!'

His eyes glinted. 'Here I am, safe and sound.'

'I was looking out for your jeep.'

He sat down beside her and lit a cigarette. 'It's the minister's car.' He glowered.

Radiance nestled up to him, and he put an arm round her shoulders. The smoke from his cigarette made her screw up her eyes, so he turned away to puff at it furiously. She realized he was angry about something.

Finally he threw away the stub and stood up. 'Now let's go and see Wu Guodong.'

'So you didn't come to pick me up!'

'Partly!' He winked at her.

They went into the hospital.

On the stairs Chen told her, 'This morning Minister Tian called up to ask me to give a talk in the ministry on my trip to Sichuan, Yunnan and Guizhou. Came to the factory himself to fetch me. But last time he convened a meeting of factory managers he didn't so much look at me. Went to everyone else's room, but not to mine. And that wasn't an oversight either.'

'What does it mean?'

Chen snorted. 'There's talk that I'm to be made a vice-minister. Tian tried to make me think that this was his doing, he was all for it. But he's secretly spreading the word that I'm ambitious, want his job, and had that article written as a publicity stunt for myself.'

'I don't want you to be a minister!'

'Why not?' Chen stopped in surprise. Radiance so seldom asserted herself.

Avoiding his eyes she murmured, 'You'd have even less time for me.'

He roared with laughter, knowing that she was afraid he'd get into trouble and make more enemies.

He stooped to take her face in his hands and kiss her.

'Don't!' she cried. 'Someone might see.'

'Is it against the law for a man to kiss his wife?' he retorted.

Radiance smoothed her hair. 'Will you take it on?'

'Not on your life! I want to make a success of our factory, and set up a Chinese motor industry to beat America and Japan in world markets.' He was talking more like a poet than a factory manager. 'Today I debunked the plan to build up industry in the interior in preparation for war. Ridiculous! Any future war will be three-dimensional, without a front line or rear. Our thinking is out of date. All the expense involved would simply be money down the drain. We've yet to end the ultra-Left line in capital construction; that's why we have fiascos like the Baoshan Steel Works and that oil-rig disaster. The bureaucrats who waste the people's money like that ought to be put on trial.'

Chen made a chopping movement with his right hand to

emphasize each sentence. His bronze face was flushed. What a man! Radiance's heart swelled with pride.

If Jade hadn't come to see Wu Guodong so often the other patients would never have believed that they were husband and wife.

She took from her bag a jar containing a mixed dish of peanuts, beancurd, chilli and lean pork. Her bag looked antiquated.

'Are you any better?'

'A little.' Wu sat cross-legged on his bed, his face as wooden as a monk meditating.

'How are the boys?' he asked.

'All right.'

Both sounded rather tongue-tied, perhaps because of the presence of other people.

Then they dried up. Jade sat motionless on her chair, her feet tucked under it like a well-behaved schoolchild.

The butcher sized her up as anaemic, the result of eating too little meat.

The arrival of Chen and Radiance was welcome. Jade stood up and offered Chen her chair. 'No you sit there,' he said, then fetched two other seats. 'I'm just back from a trip,' he told Wu. 'That's why I haven't come for so long. Any problems?'

Wu smiled punctiliously. 'No, I've no problems.'

'Good. Don't hesitate to ask if there's anything.'

'Manager Chen's so thoughtful,' Jade said to Radiance. 'He had me transferred to a job nearer home, and found our little boy a nearby kindergarten. Solved a big problem for us.'

The umbrella repairer reached for his notebook and pen.

Wu shook his head. 'I heard that the Services Bureau seized the chance to buy a truck from us.'

'That's right. We sold them one,' replied Chen.

'Isn't that against the policy? They don't come under capital construction.'

'This year we're cutting down on capital construction, so many projects have stopped or slowed down and cancelled their orders. If I can't sell our trucks how am I to pay my staff? Ask the state for loans? The state has its own difficulties. So I sell to anyone with the money to buy.' He glanced at the other patients, as if they were potential customers. 'This year we're going in for a new line – motor-bikes. There'll be a big market for them.'

Jade put in reproachfully, 'How can you talk like that, Guodong, when the manager has been so good to us.'

Chen laughed. 'Comrade Liu, you're not up to Old Wu. I like his spirit. He sticks to principle.'

Wu nodded his agreement, gratified.

Jade looked upset.

Radiance whispered to her, 'Take no notice. It's not our business.'

'Does the ministry agree to using materials allotted under the plan for products not in the plan?'

'I consulted Vice-minister Zheng.'

'What did he say?'

'He said, "Nearly all our engineering works are going to find it hard to pay their workers. With the cuts in capital investment, their products aren't in demand. And we're importing too much from abroad. We could manufacture most of the electrical equipment we need, but we don't trust our own products. In fact, our 30,000-ton hydraulic press is up to the best world standard. Well, we've just got to find our own way out. Each factory must fend for itself. Beat the foreign competition. Your factory has weathered several storms, you have experience; now's the time to show what you're made of. Maybe this setback will work out for the best. This is our chance to ditch the old methods of management. Some people will oppose change but they can't stop it. You've got to feed your workers. You'll find a way." I think Vice-minister Zheng was ab-solutely right. Now it's up to us.'

Wu frowned, the picture of doubt.

What was wrong with the old methods? Wasn't the production plan fulfilled each year?

Find their own way out? Scrap the planned economy?

Wasn't a planned economy one of the things that made socialism superior to anything else?

But he couldn't argue against the minister and his factory manager.

However, he did like the idea of outstripping foreigners. They were much hairier than Chinese. In the Party school he had learned that men had evolved from apes. Obviously foreigners were closer to apes, and the Chinese were more advanced. They should put on a spurt, as they had in the Big Leap Forward when the slogan was: Surpass England in fifteen years. Those were the days! . . . But now everything was upside down. All this talk of democracy. All the Rightists cleared. Dazhai-style* collective agriculture discredited. Free markets everywhere. Someone from his home village had told him that fortune-telling was back. This could never have happened when Chairman Mao was alive. He'd said they should have fresh cultural revolutions every seven or eight years. Yes, what was needed was military control. Those people who yelled about democracy and disrupted Chairman Mao's revolutionary line should all be thrown into gaol.

Wu looked sternly at Chen, who was eyeing the jar Jade had brought him. Wondering, no doubt, how she had flavoured the food. He took an interest in everything, did nothing by halves, so that he looked older than he really was. A striking mixture of childish ingenuousness and rich experience in the ways of the world.

All the patients had listened intently, intrigued by all Chen said.

None of the would ever meet Zheng Ziyun, but now they felt they knew him – he had expressed what was in all their hearts.

The professor remarked, 'That minister of yours is clear-headed.'

---

* Dazhai, a village in Shanxi province, was cited as a model for collective agriculture by Mao Zedong in 1964. When the move away from communes began in 1978, criticisms of Dazhai's record were voiced.

Chen glanced at his watch. 'After eight!' he exclaimed to Radiance. 'You must be famished.'

'What, haven't you eaten yet!' cried Jade in dismay. She opened the drawer by Wu's bed, but it was empty.

The professor offered them a tin of biscuits.

Chen was reaching out to take some when Radiance stopped him.

'Have you anything else to discuss with Old Wu?' she asked. 'If not, let's get home. The boys will be wondering what's happened. They know I'm not on night duty.'

'All right.' Chen turned to Wu. 'Anything I can do for you?'

'Nothing. As you're so busy don't keep coming to see me.'

All the patients stood up, as if Chen were their visitor too.

At the door of the ward the umbrella repairer said, 'Come whenever you have time!'

'I'll see,' said Chen. 'I ought to come more often, but who knows what will be waiting for me tomorrow. So long!'

14

Grace was about to make her eighth telephone call.

All she needed now was Vice-minister Kong Xiang's approval for her second daughter to stay to work in Beijing.

Grace looked at the telephone on her desk and smiled, sure of success.

Too bad the army no longer had women generals, or she could have led troops as well as any man.

Women had to be much more tenacious than men.

To other people her life seemed plain sailing. In 1945 she had joined the revolution as a singer in the northeast. At fifty-five she still had a sweeter voice than most girls of eighteen. Having joined the Party early, she had shrewdly determined to make politics her career. Starting as a secretary, she had risen to be a section chief in the Political Department. . . If it hadn't been for the Cultural Revolution she would have been a commissioner by now. So she felt life had cheated her, and often lost her temper. Her old man's stroke ten years ago had prevented him from working or being promoted. His speech was slurred, and he kept asking for delicacies to eat. Although he shuffled his feet and often stumbled, if she didn't pander to all his whims he might go to the ministry to complain about her.

Why should she be saddled with such a useless husband? He slobbered over his food, making each meal revolting. Because he was incontinent he stank. Still, she hoped he would live on, not because he was the father of her children, but because of his high monthly salary.

Who else could have put up for all these years with such an old dodderer? She'd been in her early forties when he had his stroke, though she looked in her thirties. Not for her a life of luxury, a loving husband. She had to see to everything herself, make useful connections. Other women with her qualifications could relax, relying on their husbands. Just look at her middle-school classmate Bamboo, a high official's wife.

If her old man hadn't fallen ill he would have been made a vice-minister long ago. At the time of their marriage he had been a section chief just over thirty, strong, tall and handsome. Status, good looks, ability – he'd had them all. But marriage is a gamble.

Now she was like a lioness stalking her prey each time she left home.

A knock at the door. 'Come in!' Grace called impatiently.

The door was opened cautiously. The technician from a newly designed hydro-electric station who had applied for equipment stood in the doorway, expecting another snub.

Last time he came Grace had asked as if casually, 'Does that gully of yours produce tree-ear fungus?' Tree-ear fungus was said to counteract hardening of the arteries.

'Tree-ear fungus?' He sounded as if he had never heard of it.

The dolt! Even after the Cultural Revolution, most pre-1960 college graduates had no idea how to get anything done. When the small power station in Director Feng's old home had applied for equipment, they had sent in local products. For a nominal price of course. If Director Feng hadn't introduced this fellow, Grace would have sent him packing.

She said, 'You'd better send in two more applications.'

'I'll bring them tomorrow.' He nodded repeatedly.

As Grace saw him out to the corridor she ran into Ho Jiabin, which reminded her of the voucher for a Japanese TV set issued to her section. She wanted to give it to Luo. The only person who might object was Ho.

She asked him if he wanted it, as if they had always seen eye to eye.

'I'm not wasting my money! The programmes aren't worth watching.'

Fine! She'd known he would refuse.

'Then suppose I let Old Luo have it?'

'Why him? Because he's on the Party Committee? Engineer Xin will be retiring soon. You ought to let him have it.'

What could Xin do for her? A useless old pedant who would soon be retiring?

She kept her temper though. All right, just wait! That afternoon they'd be discussing Ho's application for Party membership.

Grace dialled a telephone number.

'Hullo, who's there?'

'Secretary Cao, it's Grace.' She chuckled. She was on good terms with all the ministers' secretaries. That was the way to consolidate your position, to be kept informed of the latest developments or to pass on a message to some minister. It was important to keep in with them.

'Section Chief Li? What can I do for you?'

'I'd like to speak to Vice-minister Kong if he's free.'

'Hold on. I'll see.'

'Thanks very much.'

Grace heard the receiver put down. Then a click as the call was transferred.

'Who's that?' Kong's Sichuan drawl.

'Can't you recognize my voice, chief? What a bureaucrat! I'm Grace.'

'Ha, Young Li, still such a biting tongue. You haven't come to see me for ages.'

'Young Li indeed! My hair's white. I drop in on you each time I go to the ministry.' That was true, she never neglected to pay her respects to this Buddha. 'You're so busy attending meetings or out on trips. I've called to make a self-criticism. Ho Jiabin who wrote the article which caused such trouble is in my section. I'm to blame for not doing better political work. You should give me a dressing-down.'

'Don't worry, Young Li. That's over and done with. And you don't know the background about who was using it to get some publicity for himself. It's nothing to do with you. Just try to keep Ho in line in future.

'Remember Chairman Mao's instructions: never forget class struggle. Some people are taking the bourgeois road now, attacking the Central Committee and the Party line. That's a vicious attack on Chairman Mao, the red sun in our hearts! We should exercise proletarian dictatorship over them.'

Talk of proletarian dictatorship put fresh life into Kong. The portfolio he would have liked best was that of Public Security.

For generations his people had been poor peasants, and all his children had joined the Party or the Youth League. He had taken a Leftist stand in each political movement. True, he had been labelled as a 'capitalist roader' in the Cultural Revolution. But that didn't count.

In 1952 he had shot some capitalists and profiteers. Even Wang Fangliang and Zheng Ziyun, who outranked him, had been locked up for some months.

In 1957 he had attacked Rightists. Now, confound it,

137

they'd all been cleared and were on an equal footing with him again. This made it more difficult to uphold the Party's prestige.

In the Big Leap Forward in 1958 he'd wanted to organize the ministry like an army. When they held meetings to discuss production and the others jabbered away, he couldn't join in; but he could impose military control on them.

In the campaign to criticize Deng Xiaoping in 1976 he'd presided over dozens of big rallies. Really rousing. He always did the summing up, referring repeatedly to that 'old Rightist', 'old renegade'. Interviewed by a reporter from the *People's Daily*, he had bragged: Our criticism of Deng has boosted production, it's ten per cent higher than in 1975. Whether this was true or not he had no idea. No one would investigate.

Now Deng Xiaoping was back in power, much to Kong's indignation. All the present policies were revisionist. In the evening, drinking with old comrades-in-arms, he'd slam his wine cup down, shaking the bottle, and pour out his complaints. That fellow Deng is a Rightist – he'd better watch out!

In his office though, in the daytime, he felt deflated. When would Deng Xiaoping slip up? He was growing even more self-confident. These last two years everyone had been living in peace with no more struggle meetings, slogans, parades or pouncing on counter-revolutionaries. What was there for Kong to do? He felt uncomfortable, at a loose end.

Last year he had managed to nab a technician in the research institute. During political study this fellow had said, 'There isn't enough democracy in our Party. Some people are promoted on one person's recommendation, not elected. That's feudal.'

Kong had this statement printed and pointed out that this was a new phenomenon of class struggle.

He telephoned time and again to the Public Security Bureau, urging them to arrest that technician as a counter-revolutionary. They finally had to detain the man, but released him very soon despite Kong's protests.

When he had nothing to do, Kong recalled his impeccable past, his fine record as a Left-winger. Dreamed of the day when he would become the Minister of Public Security.

'I've a personal favour to ask too, Minister Kong.'

Grace shouldn't have broached this over the telephone. But she couldn't go to his office, where his secretary might eavesdrop. The fewer people who knew about it the better. It didn't matter going through a back door, so long as you kept it secret.

On the other hand she couldn't go to Kong's home. She had called there so frequently some years ago that his wife had finally thrown her out. That episode still rankled.

'Remember my younger daughter Niuniu?' she asked. 'She called you uncle when she was small. She'll soon be leaving college. There's a vacancy now in our research institute, and the personnel office has agreed to take her. They've sent in a request to the ministry, and say that if you approve there'll be no problem.'

'The research institute? Oh yes, I seem to remember.'

'Have you seen the request?' Grace hadn't expected such quick action.

'No. One of the section chiefs died recently, leaving three orphans. The two younger ones are still small and need looking after. The eldest is just going to graduate from college. They hope he'll be kept in Beijing.'

Grace was taken aback.

Kong shouldn't have told her this. What could she say now? And why had he sounded so offhand?

Red splotches appeared on her pale face. Tempted to slam down the receiver, she upset her teacup, splashing tea over her desk. She swept the documents off it on to the floor.

'What a hypocrite!' she thought. She had found a job in her section for Kong's son-in-law, who had never studied anything apart from class struggle. Some people had no sense of gratitude. Grace seethed with indignation.

It was because she believed in communism that she had

joined the Party, but she was a realist too. Better back down and think up more effective tactics.

Well, she would act dumb, reminding Kong not to forget her.

'Of course! Those three children really need looking after. It's easier to recruit new staff now than it was a couple of years ago. With all these new research institutes being set up, young people with genuine ability can be found jobs. If our family didn't have a real problem I wouldn't mention it. In all these years I've never asked a personal favour. You know the fix we're in with my old man ill – it's hard enough taking him to hospital, getting him up the stairs. And now as section chief I have to set an example, working hard for modernization. Can't let family problems influence my work. I don't know how to pull strings, can only depend on the leadership. You understand my position. Could you bear this in mind if an opening for your niece comes up?'

'Niuniu's forgotten her uncle. Ask her to come and see me!'

That lifted a weight from her mind.

After ringing off she sighed, then picked up her notebook and documents and mopped the desk. Under the sheet of glass on it was a photograph of her children on the Great Wall. All laughing. As tall and healthy as their father had once been. But when would they be able to do without her?

Queueing up for lunch behind Shi Quanqing, Grace whispered to him, 'Come to my office in a moment.'

What did she want? Shi couldn't enjoy his meal, just wolfed down four ounces of rice.

Had Ho Jiabin brought fresh charges against him? Had objections been raised to the subsidy he was still drawing for his son, who was already working? Had Qian told Grace how abusive he'd been about her for not raising his salary?

Grace was unpredictable. Ho Jiabin had asserted that it was her change of life.

When Shi entered her office she was weighing some tree-ear fungus which he'd got a purchasing agent to bring that morning.

Her eyes on the steelyard Grace complained, 'Each pound is one ounce underweight.'

So what? It was still a bargain.

Was this why she had called him in? He wouldn't be so ready to help her next time.

Grace took out a plastic bag for him to hold while she filled it with fungus.

She dusted off her clothes then and closed the door.

'Do you know where Luo went yesterday?' she asked.

'No.'

'To Qingdao, to fix your business.'

This staggered Shi.

Just before Liberation his father had started a mill in Shi Quanqing's name in Qingdao.

So he was a capitalist – no getting away from that. Drawing interest on his investment.

He had never admitted this. But it was discovered just before the Cultural Revolution when he applied for Party membership. So all these years he had not been admitted.

Several times Grace had put in a word for him. 'We can't judge simply by class origin.'

Guo Hongcai was adamant. Such cadres of worker-peasant origin were impossibly narrow-minded. 'It's not a question of class origin but of covering up his past. I don't think he's up to joining the Party yet.'

That was the majority view.

But in Guo's absence Grace had changed their decision to: Basically up to standard. On his return Guo had made a big scene in the Party Committee. It had been a fiasco for Grace.

Now she had sent Luo to Qingdao to smooth matters over.

Shi smiled ingratiatingly. He was thinking, 'You're not doing me a favour but trying to recruit a follower. Once I'm in I'll get even with you for the way I've been kicked around all these years. Just wait and see.'

The ministry's Party committee meeting had gone on for three whole hours. Fang Wenxuan could see that the old men were tired and bored. Most were slumped back in their chairs. Some went out to the toilet or to make telephone calls.

Grace was giving an obviously biased account of their Party branch's discussion of Ho Jiabin's application in the hope that she could induce the Party committee to exclude him.

Fang had heard about her manoeuvres, but never yet seen her in action. Not once did she glance at Feng Xiaoxian, although they were obviously in cahoots.

Feng, sitting opposite, had brewed two cups of strong tea. He was biding his time.

The others pretended to know nothing about this.

Feng's son had jeered, 'Dad, you're famous. There's an article running you down. Why don't you read it?'

So he had bought the magazine and read it from cover to cover. It struck him as counter-revolutionary rubbish about loose women and anti-Party intellectuals. Didn't Ho Jiabin make enough trouble in the ministry without raising this stink outside, mixing up with that riff-raff?

Grace's objections gave him his chance.

At least he could point out the public disapproval of Ho Jiabin's relationship to Joy.

Joy.

When Fang Wenxuan had met her at the gate that morning, she had glared instead of greeting him. He knew she was preparing for a transfer.

Was he to blame? During his last business trip, Feng Xiaoxian had arranged to transfer her to a factory in the suburbs. Fang learned of this on his return and dared not object. Joy herself, of course, was not going to ask any favours.

Now Grace and Feng were ganging up against him.

It was outrageous. What law had he broken? He had never slept with Joy, never even kissed her.

He was tempted to pound the table and make a clean breast of all his mental conflicts, his vacillation and selfishness in the past. Make it clear that he should be censured for not being a thoroughgoing materialist, not having the courage to break with old conventions. And that applied to them too.

He forced himself to keep calm.

'What public disapproval are you referring to?' he asked. 'Admitting someone to the Party is a very serious business. We must know what we're doing. Can't you be more specific, Comrade Li.'

Fang was determined to fight this out. It might be the last service he could do for Joy.

Grace was surprised by his insistence. This was not in character.

'I heard it from Guo Hongai.'

'Anyone else?'

'Shi Quanqing.'

Fang strode to the telephone, dialled a number, and asked the two of them to come to the meeting.

The old men sprawled in their chairs sat up and took an interest.

The atmosphere was tense. The minutes ticked past.

Guo came in with a foxy smile on his face.

Shi hung his head, not knowing which way to look.

Fang waited for Grace to speak. But she kept silent.

He said, 'You two told Comrade Li Ting that Comrade Ho Jiabin had an improper relationship with Comrade Wan Qun. Please elaborate on that.'

Guo replied, 'I never said that. I just said he was very good about helping her.'

The others stirred in their seats.

Fang looked at Shi.

Shi tried hard to meet his eyes but could only stare at the wall above his head. 'Once I saw Ho Jiabin leaving her place late at night.'

'What time?'

'After ten.'

'Did you see him come out of her room?'

'No, out of the building she lives in.'

'How could you be sure he'd been there and not some-where else? Quite a few of our bureau live there. I know, I've been there.' Fang rounded on Feng. 'Comrade Feng Xiaoxian, is there anything else you're not clear about?'

'What does Comrade Li Ting have to say?'

Feng was passing the buck again. But now the fat was really in the fire.

All Grace said was, 'I'll talk to Comrades Guo and Shi later on.'

Some people, caught out lying, don't even turn red. But in a woman this is doubly shocking.

Fang looked round. 'Is this cleared up then?' Everyone nodded.

'All right, then. Sorry to have troubled you.'

Guo looked eager to be questioned further, to expose Grace completely before she could settle his hash.

Shi scuttled out like a cur with its tail between its legs.

'Shall we put it to the vote now?' Fang slowly took out a cigarette and lit it.

'This needs to be further studied,' drawled Feng, frowning.

'We have studied it!' a grey-haired man rapped out.

'But we're not unanimous.' Feng stuck to his guns.

'Then the minority must abide by the majority's decision.'

Fang said vehemently, 'We're all old revolutionaries. Remember how we felt when we joined the Party. This is someone's political life. How can we exclude a good com-rade from the Party just because one or two individuals oppose him for reasons which don't bear looking into? I propose putting it to the vote.' He solemnly raised his right hand . . .

Passed!

Just then the telephone rang. As Fang took the call he turned pale. 'From the hospital. Comrade Wan Qun has been run over. They say there's no hope for her.'

Never as long as he lived would Feng forget the accusing look Fang shot at him. As if he were a murderer.

An accident can happen to anyone.

Unable to remain seated he stood up.

Feng did not believe in retribution. Still . . . if he had not had Joy transferred, if she had been sitting in her office instead of cycling, she wouldn't have been run over . . .

Seated in his car, Fang Wenxuan could not understand where he was going or why. There was nobody waiting for him, needing him. He had nothing more to hope for.

A few hours ago he had gone to see Joy for the last time. What had her dying thought been? Did she hate him or had she forgiven him?

'We've detained the driver,' the policeman in the hospital gate-house told him. He then described how the accident had happened. What was the use? She was gone for ever.

He learned from the doctor that she had died on the way to hospital. No one consoled with him. How could they know that he had lost everything that made life worth living. And he couldn't pass out or burst out sobbing. If only a sudden heart attack would save him from standing here nodding and talking, surrounded by so many people. What were they doing here? Listening to a thriller?

Hollow footsteps sounded on the stairs from the basement. Clear, detached, inexorable. The doctor took him to the mortuary.

Ho Jiabin stopped tactfully outside. If only the doctor would stay outside too.

So cold! Was she hibernating here?

25832. She was already a number. Would it be cremated with her? No, in the crematorium they would give her another.

Her body had been very carelessly cleaned up. From her flattened head her hair matted with blood was sticking up like bunches of paddy seedlings.

Her dashed-out brains had stored away more unhappy memories than happy ones. Which part contained thoughts of him? It seemed incredible that this sticky decomposing mess had produced her thoughts and feelings, had governed her whole being. Everyone must come to this, but Joy was different.

Her face looked like a lump of plasticine moulded by an impatient child and thrown away before it was finished. Her regular eyebows had disappeared. Her expressive lips failed to convey her final anguish, but were pouting like those of a child.

Why was there no chair here? He could hardly stand.

Under the narrow white sheet she seemed to have shrunk. Her gory head and mangled body spoke of the unjust fate of one who had never uttered a single word of complaint. Now she had gone, leaving him an unspoken denunciation.

Why don't you denounce and despise me, doctor, too, instead of standing by so respectfully and patiently? I have nothing more to fear, doctor. I'd like you to remember this grotesque story.

Fang Wenxuan bent down to kiss those swollen, bloody lips for the first and last time. They seemed to twitch angrily. Impossible. It was just that the tears in his eyes blurred his vision.

15

Like a presidential election in the States!

What was the point of this meeting, this specious talk? Others might be taken in, but not Wang Fangliang.

The first poll in the Ministry of Heavy Industry was 887 to 406. Zheng Ziyun was to represent them at the Twelfth Party Congress.

Tian's speech was too unctuous for words. Better go back to his office to work or read *Golden Lotus*, thought Wang. He'd managed to get an unexpurgated edition of that erotic classic.

But he couldn't leave when Tian had only just started.

Wang studied the faces in the auditorium. One plump woman was already yawning. Evidently it was contagious – her neighbour started too.

The sycophantic head of the Housing Department, in the middle of the front row, was taking notes and nodding obsequiously, as if hearing some imperial edict. Wang knew this trick. In 1958, at the Beidaihe Conference, each time he heard a sickening boast he had nodded like this and written in his notebook. Actually he was writing lampoons. Luckily, no one dared to examine his notebooks before the Cultural Revolution. Otherwise he'd have been for it.

In the old days in Yan'an, when Central Committee members made speeches, Jiang Qing had sat in front too, nodding and taking notes. He had studied in the Party school with her, had the honour of sharing the same bench and desk. In those days he had got her to sing for him. Because of that he had spent ten years in prison in the Cultural Revolution.

Tian Shoucheng was to represent G Province at this Congress. It was hardly a scientific method. How many Party members in that province knew him? A small fraction at most. Many had never even heard his name. Yet he would be speaking on their behalf. What did he know of their opinions and wishes? Were they aware that he had been a faithful follower of the Gang of Four? What did he care about the people or making the country rich and strong? All he was out for was number one.

He was trying now to discredit Zheng Ziyun by every possible means. Not simply owing to personal prejudice, but because a trial of strength was taking place between the Party's die-hards and reformers.

If Zheng were elected, there would be one more reformer who would stop at nothing.

Now Tian was putting on a show of remorse.

'Many people have joined the Party since the Cultural Revolution. Some of them were never up to the mark.

147

Some old Party members who were up to par to start with have fallen short since. I'm one.'

A buzz went through the audience. The head of the Housing Department appeared ready to burst into tears. He looked round at his neighbours, exclaiming in admiration, like one of the claque hired by old opera companies.

'I've fallen down on my job, lagged behind the times, lived as an élitist and antagonized the masses. I've analysed my faults to the Central Committee, and now I'm making a self-criticism to you all. I'm determined to mend my ways.'

Tian's voice was trembling.

The head of the Housing Department started clapping. Many others burst out too in genuine applause.

How easy it was to fool good-hearted people.

Just before this meeting Tian had fumed at his secretary Lin, 'Make me move house? No way! Where could I go? Am I to sleep in the street? Plenty of ministers have more space than me – why pick on me!'

Tian had been furious, knowing from experience that more than his housing was at stake. It threatened the whole edifice of power he had worked so hard to build up. Dark clouds were filling him with a sense of impending doom.

He had grounds for his forebodings. Since the Third Plenary Session of the Central Committee in December 1978 increasing pressure had been put on him, undermining his self-confidence. He realized that the times had changed, and he could no longer muddle through in the old way. With his powerful backing, he had once been able to weather any storm. Neither glib talk nor playing politics was any use now: you had to win the Party and people's trust by doing an honest job.

He felt hemmed in by enemies.

Nowadays a man was judged by his record in the time of the Gang of Four. When the gang fell, Tian had panicked. But when it seemed that no action would be taken against him he had announced at a mass meeting that nobody in the Ministry of Heavy Industry had been involved with the Gang of Four.

Not long after that, however, the Central Committee had criticized two vice-ministers promoted by Tian from the rank and file because their connections had enabled him to suck up to the gang.

Picking on these two men was undoubtedly an attack on him. He had tried to protect them because of his close involvement with them. But under pressure from the Central Committee he was forced to denounce them to save his own skin.

He did not keep them in isolation, alleging that the ministry had no space, so that they had plenty of chances to compare notes and make sure their stories tallied.

Each struggle meeting was a mere formality, restricted to a small group, excluding Tian's opponents. Over fifty meetings were held, but at each only one or two people read out charges. Tian had reiterated that as they were ministers who had little contact with the rank and file, they need only ask those of the rank of section chief and above to expose them. Involving more people might endanger state secrets.

He had even assured the two men at these meetings, 'Just come clean and you can keep your ministerial rank. That's what some provincial secretaries and Central Committee members have done.'

But the two men refused to cooperate. At the end of each meeting they bellowed at their accusers, 'Rubbish! Nonsense!'

Oddly enough, the work team investigating them comprised the same hacks who in 1976 had staffed first the Office for Repudiating Deng, and later the Office for Exposing the Gang of Four.

After five months or so Tian wound up this investigation, announcing, 'Our ministry had done an excellent job in exposing the Gang of Four. It's now finished. Two dozen of our staff who had connections with the gang have been investigated, and now they're in the clear.'

When the Central Committee removed these two vice-ministers from office, Tian realized that he could not get off the hook.

He had very soon been exposed. When his ministry put on an exhibition in 1976 he'd been told to make sure it stressed the repudiation of Deng Xiaoping. He had invited the heads of Qinghua University and Beijing University to see it. Then Wang Hongwen, one of the Gang of Four, had come and praised it highly. Tian had told him, 'Outsiders think we have plenty of funds and potential, but the State Planning Commission keeps cutting down on our expenditure.'

'Who in the State Planning Commission?' Wang Hongwen had asked in fury.

When Tian, feigning reluctance, named a man, Wang Hongwen had said, 'In future send your reports directly to my office.'

'We aren't qualified to write reports,' Tian had demurred.

'Never mind that. Just let me know what's happening and any problems you have. . .'

It had also emerged that it was at Tian's instigation that members of his ministry had attacked the State Council.

No use crying over spilt milk. All this had happened not long before the overthrow of the gang. Devil take it! All these years he had weathered so many storms. He could take physical hardships, but how could he bear to lose power? After Premier Zhou Enlai's death in 1976, nearly all the vice-premiers had asked for sick leave; the only one still active was Zhang Chunqiao. *

Tian thought the outcome was a foregone conclusion and felt he had backed the right horse . . .

Since then Wang Fangliang and Zheng Ziyun had upstaged him. When any problem came up they kicked over the traces or issued instructions themselves. Were they after his job?

How were the mighty fallen!

All right. He would get his own back. He could wait.

But Zheng must on no account be a delegate to the

* One of the Gang of Four. The retreat of Zhou's protégés at that point, and the dominance of the Gang of Four, persuaded Tian to believe that the safe course was to back the ultra-Left.

Twelfth Party Congress. The first poll wasn't final. It was still up to him. This might be his last chance. And all the odds were against him. But if he dragged Zheng down with him that would make his fall worthwhile.

Stick out his neck to get his head chopped off? Ridiculous.

He was not someone who could be kicked around. Just try and see!

The smug look on Tian's face reminded Wang Fangliang of an actor being given a bouquet. He wanted to shove him aside, stand up and shout, 'It's a pack of lies!'

For more than two months Tian had, with Kong Xiang's help, suppressed a Central Committee document censuring him. It was not until he was required to report the result of their investigations that Kong had shown the document to Zheng.

Zheng had been furious. 'What right had you to suppress a directive and mislead out Party Committee? This is a flagrant dereliction of duty. You must make a serious self-criticism. Have this circulated at once and call a Party meeting to decide how to handle it. Then report the outcome to our superiors.'

When Kong showed the document to each Party member, Tian's secretary Lin watched like a hawk to make sure it didn't vanish, as if it were the minutes of a Politburo meeting that they all wanted to steal to sell to foreign agents. Or as if they might copy it out and circulate it to use as ammunition against Tian . . .

Zheng wrote an open letter to the ministry's Party members, urging them to study this directive carefully and reach the right conclusions. If the Party branch took a clear, principled stand, it would help to overcome certain bad trends in the ministry, arouse the staff's enthusiasm, and contribute to unity and stability.

And the upshot? Tian stalled until Wang Fangliang and another vice-minister has gone abroad and few of the Party branch were in Beijing. He then called a meeting which proved inconclusive. No resolution was passed, and none of his manoeuvres were reported to higher authority. The fact that this directive had not been passed on to all the cadres was suppressed.

'Owing to the chaos caused by the Gang of Four, some comrades confuse right and wrong . . . Those absent from the ministry stir up trouble, those who attend their offices come under fire . . .'

This was what Tian had been leading up to all along.

It was Zheng Ziyun he was getting at.

Wang Fangliang stood up, scraping his chair, and strode across the rostrum with his hands behind his back. He was going back to his office to read *Golden Lotus*.

Wang disliked their office building. Its small windows looked like beady eyes in a fat face. The earthquake of 1976 had not even cracked it. Goodness knows how many tons of cement had gone into its foundations. The Ministry of Heavy Industry wasn't short of money.

Because the windows were so small, the lights were kept on all day in the corridor, which seemed as long as the avenue to the Ming Tombs.

Evidently quite a few people had cut the meeting. Type-writers were clacking away. In one corner he heard someone saying, 'Song Ke's luck's out this time – he's not a candidate for vice-minister.'

'Ha! He thought he'd make it by squeezing Chen Yong-ming out! By the way, is Chen on the list?' Wang stopped to hear the answer.

'I believe so.'

'Seems our Party Committee's got what it takes. Tian Shoucheng's lot may not be able to have their way.'

'Depends. Both sides are pretty evenly matched.'

'Don't be such a cynic. Since 1978 time-servers like Tian have been losing ground. The present Central Committee's not at all bad.'

'True, but there are still plenty of problems. Just take our ministry. Tian's on the attack again.'

Wang Fangliang smiled to himself. Yet his heart was warmed by their faith in the Central Committee and their understanding of current difficulties. It was a long time since he had felt so hopeful. He owed it to the people to stick it out for a few more years.

As he unlocked his office he saw Tian's second secretary Xiao Yi approach with a stack of papers.

Xiao nodded to him, then opened up Tian's office.

Xiao's trousers were always too short, and the look on his face reminded Wang of Christ on the cross – he sympathized with him.

And recently, Wang could see, the young man was looking even more agonized than ever.

In Tian's playing off of one faction against another Xiao was simply an expendable pawn.

Since the end of 1977, when the two vice-ministers had been removed from office, Tian's followers from the days of the Cultural Revolution had complained, 'Now he's crossed the river he's pulled down the bridge – he's forgotten who put him where he is.'

Plenty of accusations against him had been sent in, but they did not worry Tian. How could he lose his rank, his job, his salary, his house?

What dismayed him was that his accusers had been in his confidence.

So to undermine their prestige he boosted up the rival clique to attack their conduct during the years of turmoil.

Xiao Yi had been a nobody, born too late to join in the War of Liberation. So at the time of the Cultural Revolution he had gone all out, risking his neck to defend Chairman Mao's revolutionary line. . . Now all that was past and done with, yet here were people still settling old scores with him. Had he done wrong? Yes, he'd let himself be used to attack good comrades, and done many stupid things he now regretted.

He felt ashamed each time he saw members of the former rival rebel contingent. Why had they attacked each other as enemies? They had acted like lunatics.

Wang Fangliang stopped him. 'Comrade Xiao Yi, what's the final verdict on you?'

'That I made a serious political mistake, opposing a vice-premier,' Xiao stammered.

That put Wang's hackles up. At this rate it would soon be a crime to oppose a vice-minister! Would there never be an end to this ultra-Left lunacy!

'Did you sign that verdict?' he asked.

Xiao smiled. 'No, I can't accept it. Doesn't make sense! We've reached a deadlock.'

Wang decided to find a way out for him. He knew how to cope with Tian. Just appeal to his selfish interests and you could lead him by the nose.

The vice-principal of the Design Institute had offended Tian by criticizing him, and for three years had been assigned no work. He enlisted Wang's help. Wang asked Tian, 'Is it true that the vice-principal attacked you in the Cultural Revolution?'

Tian said cautiously, 'No, he didn't.'

With a show of surprise Wang replied, 'Then you're being wrongly accused. People say you're taking your revenge for what he did to you then!' The next day Tian had set matters right . . .

So now Wang told Xiao Yi, 'Take that verdict they've written to Minister Tian. If it's a political crime to oppose a vice-premier, ask him what opposing Vice-premier Deng Xiaoping counts as.'

Xiao Yi dumped the pile of mimeographed circulars he had just fetched on the desk. The top sheets flew away. Instead of stooping to pick them up, he kicked them into one corner.

They had no heading or signature, but each word seemed to him a provocation.

1. The Ministry of Heavy Industry already has
    elected one minister as a delegate to the
    Twelfth Congress. The two other delegates
    should not be of ministerial rank.
2. Delegates must not be over sixty-five.
3. The two other delegates should be professionals.

In the top right-hand corner was stamped 'Top Secret'.

Since they had no sense of shame, why not state outright: Forbidden to elect Zheng Ziyun.

Outrageous! In Beijing, so close to the Central Committee, in a ministry directly under the State Council. What way was this for a communist to behave?

Xiao Yi wished he could burn this pile of trash. He paced the office, arms folded. Of course it was part of the overall plot, just as was the mobilization report that Tian was now giving. To mobilize the ministry not to elect Zheng Ziyun!

His heart was palpitating. His temples were throbbing. 'Steady on!' he told himself. 'What does it matter to you who gets elected?' But then his conscience pricked him. 'Call yourself a communist? How can you take such an easy-going attitude?'

How could he let a careerist like Tian represent the ministry, and maybe even crawl into the Central Committee to abuse his power there?

Xiao Yi thumped his head with his fists.

The telephone rang.

The call was from Tian's wife. 'Is Tian there? No? Tell him to come home early. Minister H has invited us to dinner.'

Not a word of greeting or thanks, as if he were a robot.

Xiao knew Minister H, a creep.

So they were in cahoots again. Making plans for the Twelfth Congress.

Xiao Yi picked up the top circular, folded it up and put it in his pocket. The rest he left on Tian's desk in the inside office. Then he locked up and pounded down the stairs. He pedalled his rickety bike as fast as he could to Zheng's flat, like Don Quixote on his donkey imagining himself on a galloping charger.

Zheng could hardly believe his eyes. He picked up the crumpled sheet and read it again. Three distinct directions, each clearly aimed at him. He dropped the circular on a table and settled back on the sofa. The sound of a clarinet in the dusk reminded him of a horn blown at the frontier in the days of old.

He heard Bamboo come back with their grandson. She must have bought him a new toy gun. The little boy was yelling and firing his machine-gun. Zheng got up and closed the door.

Still Bamboo's voice carried clearly: 'Take your shoes off if you're climbing on the sofa.'

'Don't pull the cat's tail.'

'Oh, you naughty boy, putting the soap in the thermos flask!'

'Leave that pot of flowers alone!'

If she knew he'd just sent in his resignation again, she would make another scene. Give him no peace.

Bang! Bang! His grandson was pounding on the door.

Zheng opened it. Yes, there stood Little Fatty, legs apart, in a helmet so big that it covered his eyes. He aimed his gun at Zheng.

'Hands up, or I'll shoot you dead!'

Zheng raised both hands. 'I surrender. Now run off and play.'

With a final burst of fire the boy left in triumph.

Surrender! Zheng smiled. No way.

To free his hands to do battle with Tian, he had sent in six resignations. He had no wish to be a minister, but he had to be a delegate to the Twelfth Congress – not for the honour but for the chance to fight. Since the Third Plenary Session the ultra-Leftists and yes-men had been ganging up to make trouble, the wrong policies of the past had left a host of problems, and the people were dissatisfied with their low standard of living. Now this was being ascribed to the wrong line of the Third Plenary Session.*

Zheng's heart was very heavy.

It wasn't as if there weren't talents in the Party, people who understood economic laws and industrial management. However, lack of democracy made it impossible to get things done, forced people to tell lies, and produced opportunists like Tian who chopped and changed from day to day.

It was an extremely complex situation.

Zheng foresaw that the Twelfth Party Congress would be a big show-down between democracy, science and progress on one side and conservatism, feudalism and backwardness on the other. He had to take part in this fight to uphold the policies of the Third Plenary Session.

He had to stand up for the truth, even if it killed him. Even if he was labelled a Rightist again, a capitalist-roader. Eventually, he was sure, his name would be cleared. He might not live to see it. But society was bound to move ahead.

For Zheng the Third Plenary Session was just as important in the history of the Party as the Zunyi Conference during the Long March.** Although so brief, it had reached many major decisions. Had introduced agricultural and economic reforms to raise living standards. The righting of wrongs, the rehabilitation of Rightists and the correction of the wrong policy towards intellectuals had helped to arouse the enthusiasm of millions. So it had to be recognized as a turning-point in China's socialist construction.

Zheng was determined to tackle Tian.

Tian Shoucheng was surprised to find Zheng sitting in his office. It reminded him that as he came in Xiao Yi had looked unusually grave.

---

* The Third Plenary Session of the 11th Party Congress held in December 1978 at which significant changes in policy were announced.
** A conference held in January 1935 at which Mao became Party leader and guerilla tactics were readopted.

This spelt trouble.

'Feeling better?' he asked placidly. 'Why not take a longer rest?'

'Sit down!' said Zheng, then picked up the crumpled circular on the table. 'Can you explain what this means, Comrade Tian Shoucheng?'

Tian stared for a while at the circular, as if he were a foreigner only just learning Chinese. 'Where did you get this?' he asked.

'That's immaterial. As vice-secretary of our Party branch and a vice-minister I've the right to ask this question.' Zheng lit a cigarette without looking at Tian.

He had plenty of time.

In the silence that followed, Tian could hear his heart pounding. Since there was no avoiding this confrontation he would just have to brazen it out. 'The idea is to have a broader representation, so that our delegates can speak for the masses . . .'

'Was this passed by the Party branch?'

Tian took out a cigarette too, but his lighter failed to work. Zheng chucked him his box of matches.

Tian inhaled a puff of smoke. 'In a small-group discussion.'

'Show me the minutes.' Zheng held out his right hand. A frown flickered over Tian's oily face.

'Oh . . . it was just a . . . private discussion.'

'How many of you? Who else was there?' Zheng walked over to confront him.

There was no answer.

'A private discussion, yet you draw up a circular in the name of the Party Committee. Who gave you the right to break the Central Committee's rules on the election of Party delegates? No wonder the rank and file say the Ministry of Heavy Industry is run by four people, not by the Party Committee.' Zheng stubbed out his cigarette and threw it into an ashtray. Tian did not have to tell him who the others were.

'We didn't use the Party Committee's official stamp,' countered Tian.

'Why didn't you have the guts to sign your names? I want you to call a meeting to explain this flagrant breach of discipline. It isn't the first time you've bypassed the Party Committee. To say one thing in meetings then to act quite differently is no way for a communist to behave.'

He was talking very big, but then he wanted to be elected. Maybe he even hoped to be made an alternate member of the Central Committee. That was why, although so ill, he refused to rest but had worn himself out making speeches right and left, calling for reforms. He was always muscling in, harping on making their work more scientific. Some of the higher-ups liked that talk. Was it paving the way for his election to the Central Committee? The hypocrite!

But Tian kept his temper. 'If you disagree, we can discuss it,' he said. 'Don't let personal prejudice get the better of you. In your state of health you shouldn't fly off the handle.'

He must quieten Zheng down. The fellow would stop at nothing. After all these years in office, he was still like a new football player ignorant of the rules of the game. Better keep out of his way or he might knock you down.

Zheng knew what Tian was driving at. Knew the way his mind worked. He smiled.

'Don't change the subject. Let's stick to the point. This business has got to be settled right away. Either you revoke that circular, or I'll report it.'

Really a 'stone in a latrine, hard and stinking'. That was how someone had described Zheng Ziyun in the early days of the Cultural Revolution. Dead right too.

'If you insist, we'll reconsider.'

Reconsidering. That would provide time for more manoeuvring . . .

'Very well, I'll wait to hear from you.' Zheng had to leave Tian a way out.

After seeing Zheng out, Tian picked up the crumpled circular, tore it up and chucked it into the wastepaper basket.

Zheng had won another round, damn it.

But Tian had patience. He would bide his time till Zheng slipped up. His chance was sure to come. Then he would be fully as ruthless as Zheng and go on to the offensive.

Nonetheless, Tian felt that all his recent setbacks had been owing to bad judgement. He was losing his grip, past his prime. He and Zheng were about the same age, yet Zheng in spite of his illness still had drive.

Tian sipped some tea. It was bitter, too strong, but refreshing. He slowly drank more. The last couple of years he had taken to drinking strong tea. Nowadays he needed stimulants – strong tea, tobacco, liquor. He glanced at the table. Sure enough, Zheng had not touched his tea . . . The man ought to have been a monk!

Looking up, Tian noticed Xiao Yi in the doorway. How long had he been standing there? Was he spying on him? Luckily science wasn't yet so advanced that you could read people's thoughts.

Xiao had a strange expression on his face. As if he had something to say, yet was hesitant to speak.

'What is it, young Xiao?'

The fellow was a nuisance standing there.

'It's like this,' Xiao Yi stammered. 'I didn't like to interrupt when you were talking to the deputy minister. Didn't you ask where he got that circular? Well, I gave it to him.'

Tian could see what an effort this admission cost. Xiao looked ready now to decamp. Tian had seen from the start that Xiao had never wanted to be his secretary and felt ill at ease with him.

But he wasn't going to let him go. He didn't want word of this to get around. In the last few years he had sized Xiao Yi up as someone completely unworldly. He couldn't have been more mistaken. Must guard against him.

Weighing his words he said, 'Comrade Xiao Yi, what you did disrupted unity and stability. Well, we'll say no more about it. Be more careful in future.'

'It wasn't what I did but this whole business that has

disrupted unity and stability,' Xiao Yi retorted. 'Any decent communist would oppose it. And I'd like to be transferred to another job. I'm not up to my present work.'

So! Tian decided there was no point in trying to justify himself.

'It was for the sake of the work,' he pontificated. 'But we can discuss that later.'

When Xiao Yi had left, Tian felt that his morning had been wasted, people were conspiring against him.

A man in his position had a hard life!

Still, you had to pay a price to get what you wanted. His gains still outweighed his losses.

16

More than two hours had passed since supper. All that time Zheng and Bamboo had been sitting waiting for Yuanyuan, ready to pounce on her when she came in.

Bamboo kept looking at her watch every minute, then sighing, pressing her hands to her heart and glaring at the photographs on the tea table. She must have searched Yuanyuan's drawers again – she was impossible.

In one picture Mo Zheng was whispering in Yuanyuan's ear while she leaned on his shoulder, eyes narrowed, head thrown back. Had the sun dazzled her eyes?

Another showed them hand in hand, walking towards the horizon where the sun was setting. The evening breeze had ruffled the grass and leaves; the vast plain seemed deserted.

There was one of Yuanyuan stuffing an ice-lolly between Mo Zheng's lips, laughing as he tried to dodge . . .

They were good shots. Yuanyuan must have posed them. Wasn't she a professional photographer? They were fresh and stylish. . . Yet none of her photographs had yet been published. She always said, 'I can never get good shots.'

Probably, like her father, she set herself high standards, unwilling to submit work she thought mediocre.

As soon as Zheng arrived home, Bamboo had rushed at him, brandishing these pictures. 'Look what your precious daughter has done!'

His daughter? Whenever Bamboo disapproved of Yuanyuan's behaviour she became *his* daughter.

Was what Bamboo told him true? She must have checked up – she had nothing else to do.

'Mo Zheng was arrested for stealing. He's the adopted son of that woman reporter of yours.' Bamboo sounded rather exultant.

So Autumn, too, had become *his*.

Zheng frowned, anxious to avoid another scene.

The photographs showed how close Mo Zheng and Yuanyuan were. This came as less of a shock to him than to Bamboo.

Yuanyuan had already given him a hint.

He was suffering from insomnia one night when finally he heard her door-key. He jumped up and went to meet her, his grey hair ruffled, his pyjamas crumpled, a jacket draped over his shoulders.

Yuanyuan braced herself for a scolding.

'Have you had supper? We've got pot-stewed duck's feet.' He smiled coaxingly, eager to keep her up.

'Really?' Yuanyuan arched her dark eyebrows, so like his own.

He waited patiently while she hung up her big duffle bag, kicked off her high-heeled shoes and changed into slippers.

Having watched her wash her hands he followed her to the kitchen to find the dish of duck's feet. 'I've had supper,' she said. 'Still . . .'

She hooked out a stool for him from under the table, then another for herself. They both sat down.

'Mum been on about me again?' she mumbled with her mouth full.

'No.'

Yuanyuan smiled sceptically, sucking the greasy fingers of her left hand, one by one.

162

'Dad, if I fell in love, could you trust my choice?'

This caught Zheng off guard. He felt like a lonely old man starved of affection.

He was often stumped by Yuanyuan's capricious questions.

At heart he trusted her. She took life seriously, could use her head, though she always struck others as flippant. But this was something that would affect her happiness for life. Could she have been carried away by her feelings? Love could be quite irrational.

'You're talking in riddles, Yuanyuan. Giving me nothing to go on. Maybe you think I'm a fuddy-duddy. We're the products of different times. First I did underground work, then joined the ministry . . . So it's facts I go by. You must tell me what he's like. Otherwise how can I say? Do you really have someone?'

'Not yet.' Yuanyuan smiled. 'But some day.'

'Will you tell me then?'

'Of course!' She sprang up to kiss his forehead. 'Dear dad, no one understands me the way you do.'

'Of course', indeed. The little schemer.

Apart from these photographs, Zheng was in the dark.

Caught off guard again.

He studied the pictures intently. If the boy hadn't been arrested he was obviously lovable. Why else would Autumn have adopted him? Or Yuanyuan fallen for him? Were they sillier than Bamboo? He found this puzzling.

Zheng had never seen Yuanyuan smiling as she was in these photographs. He sighed. That smile was uniquely hers.

It didn't belong to the mother who had borne her, the father who had brought her up. Yes, they had borne and brought her up, and now this young fellow had stolen her away.

Bamboo said sternly, 'You must have this out with her.'

Easier said than done.

'Don't get worked up,' he warned her. 'That might get us into a deadlock.'

'You spoil her, always letting her have her own way.

That's why it's come to this.' Looking round, Bamboo saw that the curtain hadn't been drawn. She yanked angrily at the cord, then tugged at the curtain.

When he went over to help, she pushed his hand away, tore the curtain down, and trampled on it.

Hysterical!

Zheng sat down without a word, his lips compressed. These constant scenes got him down. Some people found it so easy to ruin their own lives and those of all around them. The torn curtain on the floor looked like a balloon that had burst, faded and dusty.

Mo Zheng was driving his motor-bike fast. Yuanyuan rested her head on his broad back.

She was tired out. Blissfully tired. She closed her eyes, forgetting where they were going. What did it matter? She would go with Mo Zheng to the ends of the earth. She smiled and held her right hand to his lips.

He turned to kiss her small hand, as rough as a boy's. Because of her, the street lamps ahead had turned into gems, his motorbike into a boat crossing a channel.

Mo Zheng believed he could make it. Because he felt responsible for this girl, lovely as a flower, who had so unreservedly entrusted herself to him. By giving him her love she had washed him clean – his little Virgin Mary!

He felt as if he were making a new start in life.

As if she knew his thoughts, Yuanyuan tweaked his ear, then told him, 'I want to lean on your back all my life.'

He smiled feeling her warm breath on his ear.

His heart, which had been like and old tree blasted by lightning, had now put forth new boughs and soft green foliage. Its leaves would sough in the wind, would provide shelter for hungry, thirsty travellers . . . He loved this world more than ever, loved his fellow creatures. Even if lightning struck again his roots went deep, drawing nourishment from Mother Earth. Years later new boughs would grow. The cycle of life and death would never end.

Mo Zheng was ashamed now of his past despair, resentment and self-pity.

Yuanyuan tiptoed into the flat. Strange, the sitting-room lights were on. Wasn't her mother watching TV this evening?

She picked up the little mirror on her table. It reflected a lovely stranger: darker eyebrows, brighter eyes and rosier cheeks.

She pouted, then smiled, disclosing small, white, even teeth. All his!

She was in love!

With a laugh she flung herself on her bed and buried her face in the pillow. She had promised to marry him.

Marriage! The idea was frightening. The big doll on her bookcase stared at her disapprovingly as if to ask, 'Are you giving up your girlhood so lightly?'

Yuanyuan sprang up to face the doll, exclaiming softly, 'You'll never understand!'

How could it understand that when two people became one it was not a loss but a gain. They would use their heads, their hands, to build a new life.

Mo Zheng had said he would never live with her family or leave Autumn, who had been mother, elder sister and friend to him. After he married Yuanyuan he could care for Autumn better. And when they had a child they would teach it to call her 'Granny'. Yuanyuan had hidden her face to laugh. He intended to become a good translator, to make that his profession. Yuanyuan had shaken her head. But in fact he had already translated three stories which Autumn had promised to show to an old classmate, the editor of a literary magazine.

The two of them had agreed that if those stories were published they would use the payment to buy their first new quilt, a quilt with a sapphire silk cover . . .

'Yuanyuan!' A shriek from Bamboo aroused Yuanyuan from her dreams.

'What is it?'

'Come here. Your father and I want to talk to you.'

It sounded like trouble.

Yuanyuan smoothed her ruffled hair with a final glance at the mirror, then went reluctantly to the sitting-room.

She shot a glance at her parents. Something was up, that was certain.

Zheng saw her compress her lips. A bad sign. Before the subject was broached, her back was up.

'Sit down!' Bamboo spoke as she would to some refractory subordinate. 'Go on, Zheng.'

It was a delicate subject. How could he avoid hurting Yuanyuan's feelings. How could he persuade her to give up this man?

Why should people fall in love? It complicated life. Tears, love letters, dates, pledges – such an expenditure of time and energy. Love's rightful place was in fiction. He and Bamboo had never been in love, yet they had lived together all these years.

He tried to ease the tension. 'You seem very busy, Yuanyuan, these days, not coming home for supper . . .'

Yuanyuan shrugged. He had made a false start. Better not beat about the bush.

'Your mother and I are very concerned about you. By a certain age everybody wants to get married. When considering a future husband, the main criteria should be his political stand, his character, his attitude to his job . . .' Hell, even to him this sounded like a formal speech. No, his speeches were livelier than this. Yuanyuan seemed to be suppressing a pitying, sarcastic smile.

Bamboo was glaring at him impatiently.

Zheng made an effort to describe his ideal son-in-law.

Yuanyuan laughed.

'Dad, you make it all sound like choosing a pair of shoes in a shop.'

'Don't talk that way, Yuanyuan. That's enough, Zheng.' Bamboo pulled the photographs from behind her back. 'In future, I'm telling you, you're not to bring pictures of this man here. You're to break with him at once!'

Yuanyuan rushed forward. Bamboo sat on the pictures.

'Mum you're a spy!' Yuanyuan's face, flushed a moment ago, was white. 'What right have you to search my room? That's against the Constitution. Give me back those pictures.'

Her voice, like Bamboo's, had risen.

'Give them back!?' Bamboo tore up the pictures and tossed them in a spittoon. 'Spy, indeed! How dare you! Cuddling up to a man in a picture before you're married – have you no sense of shame?'

'Bamboo!' Zheng could not stand for this.

Yuanyuan's anger had subsided. 'All right, tear them up, I'll take more. Cheek by cheek and kissing each other. I'm going to marry him. It's none of your business.'

Bamboo slapped her face, leaving five red finger-marks. 'Shameless hussy!' Heavens, had she forgotten her own affair with another man? Zheng had never sworn at her like this. Yet now she was behaving like an avenging fury.

'You'll be sorry for this!' Yuanyuan had never before felt such hatred.

Zheng knew then that Bamboo had lost this daughter. His darling daughter. He pushed his wife aside. 'How could you!' he protested. 'That's enough. We'll talk about it tomorrow.' He started steering Yuanyuan out of the room.

'Hey, you nearly pushed me over. You're ganging up against me. No, we must get this thrashed out today. Yuanyuan, you're living off me. I brought you up. Why are you disobeying me and making me so angry?'

'You chose to have me. It was your duty to bring me up. I owe you nothing.'

Bamboo grabbed up a stool and charged. Zheng was unable to stop her.

Yuanyuan snatched the stool away and hurled it into a corner. The tenants downstairs rapped on the radiator.

'Want to fight? You dare!' screamed Bamboo, hurtling towards Yuanyuan.

'Do keep your voices down. What will people think?'

Yuanyuan gave Bamboo a shove that sent her staggering. 'Come off it, I'm not fighting you – that's a lie.'

'Get out of here, you're no daughter of mine!' Bamboo spluttered, beside herself with rage.

Zheng closed his eyes. She looked such a revolting sight.

'Don't take it to heart, Yuanyuan. Your mother doesn't know what she's saying.' Once more he steered his daughter towards the door.

'Of course I'm going. I've always wanted to leave this hateful, hypocritical home. Think I care about your status, your flat, or your standard of living? I was sorry for dad, that's all. But, dad, you're a hypocrite too. You know mum's faults and despise her. You only come here to sleep, and shut yourself in your office as much of the time as you can. When you do come home you go straight to your own room. In front of visitors, though, you pour tea for her, fetch her a chair, help her on with her coat and open the door for her like a devoted husband. Well, you can't fool me. Does she love you? No, only herself. Has she ever lost sleep worrying about you? All she cares about is your position, your car, your good flat, your perks as a minister. If she weren't a minister's wife could she go on drawing her salary month after month without doing a stroke of work? You have all those fine clothes, mum, silks and satins. Look what dad wears – does he dress like a minister?' Yuanyuan turned up Zheng's padded jacket to show that the lining was torn. 'If you won't buy him a new one, you might at least mend this or get Mrs Wu to do it. But that wouldn't occur to you, would it? I've even seen you burn his arm with your cigarette and box his ears. You're a psychopath. Dad would hate losing face if anyone knew, so you can get away with it.'

Yuanyuan turned to Zheng. 'I know her, I've no illusions about her. But you . . . You believe in making political work scientific, in behaviourism, concern for other people – yet you won't believe in Mo Zheng. What's stealing? Taking something that doesn't belong to you. Well, that means mum's salary is stolen: she never goes to the office. I refuse to live in your hypocritical way. Mo Zheng and I are going to live like real human beings. We love and respect each other. We're going to make our own way in life. Don't worry, even if the sky falls I won't come begging for charity. That's all I have to say. I'm off now.'

Zheng sat by Yuanyuan's desk watching her pack. He could say nothing to keep her, for it seemed to him right for her to leave. He knew how much he would miss her, otherwise he would have been glad for her sake.

Yuanyuan had calmed down. She felt no further obligation to this family. She tossed aside the expensive blue anorak and put an old padded jacket over her jumper. Its sleeves were too short for her and it was tight. Over it she put a bigger corduroy jacket.

Zheng knew that she was not taking anything bought by Bamboo. And that she would never go back on her word. He fetched an old padded overcoat from his room and held it out to her. 'Put this on. It's so cold, and you're always riding that motor-bike.'

'No, I shan't be cold.'

'It's mine.' His voice was trembling.

Yuanyuan took the coat, buried her face in it and burst into tears, turning away from him the way she had as a child when crying. 'Forgive me, dad,' she sobbed. 'I really can't stand it here.'

Zheng felt ashamed. It was his fault that she had been born into a home like this. He was powerless to help her, had just taken part in humiliating her.

He took Yuanyuan in his arms and stroked her curly bobbed hair. When was the last time he had done this? How quickly she had grown up and he had aged. 'There, there, I'm the one who should be asking forgiveness.'

The rear light of the motor-bike had disappeared. Still Zheng stood, dazed, in the cold wind.

Was it his voice pleading, 'Yuanyuan, don't go, don't leave me all alone'?

Why had he not said this to her? For fear she might ask, 'What is there to keep me here?'

He would have had no answer.

169

She had been right, he was a hypocrite. She was probably the only one, apart from himself, who knew this. She had exposed him completely.

To keep up appearances he had compromised, put up with everything. Even Bamboo's unfaithfulness to him in her young days. He was well aware that Fangfang – ruthless, vulgar, politically backward – was not his daughter. Did he make allowances for Bamboo because he loved her? No. She had long since forfeited his love and respect. He had wanted, selfishly, to improve his image. He could talk in a scientific way and understood Marxist theories, yet his own conduct was governed by old conventions.

Why was he so concerned about his image? Behind his devotion to the cause lurked a hankering for fame. He ought to admit that this was why he had suppressed his instincts and natural desires.

He lacked Yuanyuan's courage. She had opted for freedom.

The wind was rising, freezing him to the marrow of his bones. He had never before felt so lonely.

He trudged on aimlessly.

It began to snow. The big snowflakes whirling through the air reminded him of small white butterflies.

Butterflies!

When Yuanyuan was six she had been in hospital to have her tonsils out. He had sat for hours by her small white bed. Had listened to her even breathing, watched her chubby face and felt responsible for her and her whole generation.

Waking, she had asked, 'Where's mama?'

'She's busy. Hush, don't talk.' That was the first time he had lied to Yuanyuan. How could he tell her that her mother was dancing in Beijing Hotel?

'Tell me a story, daddy.'

'What kind of story?' He had racked his brains for one.

Yuanyuan had stared at him, disappointed. What bad parents we are, he had thought, a father who can't tell stories and a mother who goes dancing while her little girl is in hospital.

'Daddy, where do butterflies come from?'

'Caterpillars turn into butterflies.'

'Don't be silly!' Yuanyuan couldn't believe that an ugly caterpillar could turn into a lovely butterfly.

She had probably forgotten this long ago. He had only just recalled the incident.

Even after a painful metamorphosis, not all caterpillars turned into butterflies. Some died as larvae.

He was still in that stage.

In his heart he told his daughter, 'You mustn't think too highly of me. Accept me as a caterpillar, going through a painful metamorphosis but liable to die before I turn into a butterfly.'

He ought to tell her this to her face. Mo Zheng, too, whom he had wronged before even meeting him.

What time was it? Nearly eleven. The last bus hadn't yet left.

Jade yawned. Her legs felt wooden as she dragged herself upstairs.

Tomorrow was New Year's Day. These last few days she'd been busier than ever. So many women had wanted perms that she'd worked from 8 a.m. to 10 p.m., hardly able to stand by the time she'd finished.

What had Little Qiang had for supper? That morning she'd fried him two dishes and left them in the steamer with some buns. She'd put water in the pan on the stove. He had only to light the gas. But Autumn was sure to have taken him to her flat to eat. Jade didn't like to put her to so much trouble. She had many times offered to give her a stylish perm to make her look a bit more presentable.

But Autumn always declined.

Jade stopped halfway upstairs to catch her breath. Was that groaning? Sounded very close. She went on up and found an elderly man sprawled on the stairs.

'What's wrong, comrade?' She tried to lift him up.

Zheng Ziyun opened his eyes and motioned her back, pointing to some white pills scattered on the stairs.

Jade promptly picked a few up and put them in his mouth. Then she knocked on Autumn's door and called for her.

The door opened on three smiling faces: Autumn, Mo Zheng and the pretty Yuanyuan who often called on them.

'Quick, someone's collapsed on the stairs. Looks bad.' Jade was frantic.

They hurried downstairs after her.

'Dad!' Yuanyuan rushed to him.

'Old Zheng! Quick, Mo Zheng, call a taxi.'

Zheng opened his eyes as if he had reached the terminus.

It seemed too dramatic, meeting Mo Zheng this way. He hoped the young man and Yuanyuan would not suppose he had come to make a scene.

Yuanyuan burst into tears of remorse, blaming herself for her father's heart attack.

'Don't cry,' said Autumn sternly. 'Don't shake him, he needs quiet. Keep him still.' She knelt to put an arm under Zheng's head. 'Go and get a pillow.'

Yuanyuan was too dazed to move. Jade hurried off for a pillow.

Why did it take so long to get a cab? Autumn feared that every second's delay might prove fatal. Beads of sweat broke out on her head.

He musn't be allowed to die. China had too few men of his calibre.

Yuanyuan pressed her cheek against her father's cold, clammy hand. 'Dad, I promise to love you better. Please forget all I said. Dear dad, I understand you. . .'

'Don't talk, Yuanyuan. Let him be quiet,' Autumn snapped.

At last the taxi came.

Mo Zheng carried Zheng out.

How strong his arms were! The young man's vitality put fresh strength into Zheng. He felt like a child in a giant's arms. Don't worry, he wouldn't die. Zheng opened his eyes and found Mo Zheng's brilliant pupils fixed on him. The magnetism of his gaze drew back a life fast ebbing away.

Zheng tried to smile at him. How fine it would be to have such a son.

Epilogue

The telephone rang.

Confound it, waking him up so late at night.

Tian Shoucheng opened his eyes. The phone went on ringing insistently – maybe it was some urgent business. He sat up and felt for his slippers on the floor. Damn it, he had put his right foot into his left slipper.

'Well?' he snapped impatiently.

'Excuse me, Minister, for disturbing you.' It was Ji Hengquan trying to butter him up.

'What's up?' Tian drawled. He could hear Ji swallowing, as if a tasty dish in front of him was making his mouth water.

'Minister Zheng has had a heart attack and been rushed to hospital, Ji sounded tense, to hide his inward glee.

'Oh!' Tian was suddenly wide-awake. 'What happened?'

'It was at that woman reporter's place, they say. After eleven this evening.' Ji gabbled this off, as if afraid he might drop dead before broadcasting this news. Or like an agent coming back from the enemy camp in a film with sheaves of intelligence, to report exultantly on the success of his mission.

'Ah – ' Tian's voice slid down the scale. 'Be sure and tell the hospital that I want him to have the very best care and medicine, with the best doctors and nurses in attendance . . . Comrade Zheng Ziyun is highly respected in economic circles. He must be saved. The country can't spare him . . . Where are you now? In the hospital? Good, I'll come straight over.' Tian sounded immensely concerned, consumed by anxiety.

As he rang off, the result of the last vote for a delegate to the Twelfth Congress flashed through his mind: 1,006 to 287.

When Tian had gone to such pains to draw up those three regulations for electing delegates contrary to the Central Committee's rules, Zheng Ziyun had seized on the chance to do him down. The result was that Zheng's vote had risen from 887 to 1,006. Tian had gambled and lost.

That had taken the wind out of his sails. But now, suddenly, the tables had been turned.

Well, now Zheng Ziyun could not attend the Twelfth Congress.

Tian seated himself more solemnly than usual in his limousine. Late as it was, not a hair of his head was ruffled. He was dressed as neatly as if going to a banquet.

He bent to look at the luminous dial of his watch. It was 3.41 a.m., January 1 1981.

But he was in for a surprise. The doctor on duty told him that Zheng was out of danger. Splendid, everybody should live to be a hundred. However, Tian felt more exhausted than ever before in his life. The battle would have to go on.

Afterword

Zhang Jie is one of the most interesting writers to emerge in China in the last ten years. In much of her work, like other women writers of her generation, she is concerned with subjects such as love and marriage in Chinese society. She exposes the generally negative attitudes towards divorce which lead many couples to continue hypocritically in unhappy relationships because they fear the public condemnation which a breakup would produce. She shows particular sympathy for the female victims of repressive social attitudes and attacks the misogynist morality of feudal tradition. In her novella, *The Ark*, she explores with real sympathy the problems of three divorced women who try to build independent lives, showing the stress that social pressures put them under. That story was acclaimed (and attacked) as a feminist work.

In *Leaden Wings* Zhang Jie takes the development of heavy industry in China as her main theme. This is a statement in itself as it is not a usual subject for a woman writer to tackle. She does so with authority because she has considerable work experience in industry. As Zhang is seen as a strong and assertive woman writer it is natural that we should look at her women characters with special interest. In *Leaden Wings*, however, the women characters shock or disappoint more than they inspire. It is worth considering why this is so.

Autumn, the reporter, unlike the other female characters, is both good and strong. She is outspoken and principled, a journalist who believes in what she writes, bravely, although perhaps not voluntarily, leading a celibate life in a marrying society. She pays a heavy price for her independence. She has no outlet for her love other than her adopted son, yet she is gossiped about behind her back by those who believe she is divorced and equate divorcees with prostitutes. Nor is she able to rise above all this. She is ugly and cares about it. Zhang Jie asserts 'nothing is more agonizing for a woman than ugliness'. Despite her integrity, many people see Autumn as a ridiculous misfit. She is aware of this and the knowledge forces her to be more conformist. Zhang Jie doesn't condone this view of Autumn but does, I think, encourage us to see her as somehow incomplete and wasted. She is certainly not presented as a role model.

Apart from Autumn, the women in *Leaden Wings* are either strong and evil or good but rather weak. First among the 'bad' women is Bamboo, the spoilt lazy wife of Vice-minister Chen. She is arrogant and rude, very materialistic and apparently has no real affection for anyone. Her husband is shown as the prisoner of their unhappy marriage, while she is allocated the role of its architect. We see the failure of their relationship through his eyes.

> [Marriage] had to be tended carefully, like plants. A marriage wasn't a broom to be brought home and tossed behind the kitchen door. Women who failed to understand this were fools.

We do not get Bamboo's version. Later he reproaches her,

> 'You're so morbidly suspicious of all other women. Have you no self-respect? I can't understand women like you. On International Women's Day you shout about the emancipation of women. But at home you depend on your husbands like feudal wives. Political and economic equality isn't enough. Women have got to emancipate themselves.' He stopped, eyeing her hair and clothes. 'You should get ahead, win your husband's respect. Not just doll yourselves up. . .'

She cries but again is not allowed a reply.

Greedy, vain and domineering towards her daughter, Bamboo is a character whom the reader is meant to dislike.

176

We are left to reflect for ourselves that the position of the wife of a senior politician whose status and job depend on him is not an easy one. No attempt is made to explore the social forces which make Bamboo what she is.

Grace is preferable to Bamboo only in that she is a tough, independent woman. Like Bamboo who was her classmate at school, Grace puts a lot of energy into pulling strings for her daughter. She is malicious and bears grudges. Her plotting and manoeuvring at work are all in defence of narrowly-conceived self-interest, yet she is self-righteous and smug. She is disliked, even by her protégé for whom she is trying to obtain Party membership. She does at least believe in her own ability and apparently in that of her sex. 'Women,' she muses, 'have to be more tenacious than men.' Yet it is clear that her self-reliance has been thrust upon her, she hankers after a more dependent life, envying Bamboo who can relax and rely on her husband.

Grace is burdened with an incontinent invalid husband, a fact which we discover through her complaints. We are not invited to sympathize with her or to excuse any of her faults in the light of her misfortunes, on the contrary we are supposed to find her resentment shocking. To make sure that we do, we are told that she wishes her husband to live, only in order that the family may continue to receive his high salary.

The bleak characterization of these two female characters contrasts with Zhang Jie's treatment of her male villains who are the conservatives in the policy struggle which is taking place in the Ministry of Heavy Industry. Zhang Jie's stand in this struggle is quite clear. The conservatives from the minister downwards have no valid argument against the reforms they are so unhappy about; they oppose change because they fear it may disturb their own comfortable niches. The reformers on the other hand are not out to make a career for themselves, they just wish to modernize Chinese industry. Yet with the men, Zhang has avoided the crude division into positive and negative characters which was officially demanded of literature in the 1960s and 1970s and is not unusual even today. The motives of her male villains are comprehensible. They are not likeable but can be pitied for their paranoid fears. Her 'good' men are balanced by their flaws. Vice-minister Zheng is to be admired at work, but he lives a lie at home. His ally, Wang Fangliang, is a cynic who turns to an erotic novel for light relief. Ho Jiabin, honest and outspoken, has an ethereal quality which makes it hard even for his friends to take him seriously.

The good women in the novel are all 'nice', an adjective which is not particularly appropriate for the good men. There is Joy, the pathetic widow who meekly accepts the hard deal she has received from life, struggling to bring up her son on her own after her husband's suicide. In her rather passive resignation to her fate she demonstrates traditional Chinese feminine virtues rather than the qualities of a modern heroine. Her death in a tragic accident merely confirms her status as a victim.

Radiance, the doctor wife of Chen Yongming, is at least shown as having independent status in her job at a hospital. She is not specially talented, but is a thoroughly conscientious doctor, devoted to her patients. Yet we are left in no doubt that her factory manager husband, for whom she feels a rather cloying admiration, is the mainspring of her life. No politician, she never attempts to interfere in his work but makes his life easier by her 'wifely concern' for his health and comfort. She is happy because she has the 'strong husband to look up to' of whom she had dreamed as a girl.

Jade, the hairdresser, has a busy life too. Her husband is in hospital so that as well as her full-time job she must cope with their two children and all the domestic responsibilities unaided on a reduced budget. She is a good mother, a dutiful wife, and kind, despite her exhaustion, to her customers. She seems saddened by her husband's severity but understands that realistically her only choice is to resign herself to it.

Her husband neither smoked nor drank. Each month he made over all his pay to her. He didn't laze about, leaving her all the housework. Nor did he insist on scrambled eggs and two ounces of liquor for supper while she and the children ate cornmeal muffins and cheap pickles. He wasn't a bad man. What exhausted her was the way he kept nagging.

Again we seem to be looking at a victim who can accept her life as it is only because her expectations are not high.

So why are there no more positive female characters in *Leaden Wings* and why did Zhang Jie paint such cruel portaits of middle-aged women of the official class? Perhaps to understand this we must think again about what she is doing. She repeatedly attacks the conventions of marriage as it exists now in China, but she appears to see a 'good' relationship with a man as the best guarantee of happiness for a woman. Radiance's relationship with Chen does not leave a western feminist very comfortable, but Zhang may well see it as ideal. Autumn is a victim of the system. Zheng's thoughts may stray towards her but he can never risk the scandal which would ensue if he left his wife. Joy suffers in the same way because Fang Wenxuan, who loves her, can't divorce the woman who betrayed him. Jade is making the best of things because as a married woman with two children she really has no other option.

Grace and Bamboo are singled out for such ferocious treatment because they are the gatekeepers who uphold the morality which Zhang Jie sees as so oppressive to its victims. In China, as in many societies, it is middle-aged women who, having achieved a place in their society, do all they can to ensure the preservation of that society's moral and social order by the means at their disposal. The fact that society may be manifestly unfair to their sex does not affect the behaviour of such women because they have so assimilated its values. Frequently less socially secure than the men, they are likely to be publicly more conformist.

Zhang Jie, herself a divorcee for many years, no doubt suffered insults and gossip about her private life. Her merciless depiction of Bamboo and Grace should be understood as an attack on the many priggish and hypocritical busybodies of their type who make other's people's lives a misery or even ruin their careers by gossip and innuendo which can be extraordinarily damaging in a puritanical society.

Although she is concerned with women's predicament and with issues like marriage and divorce which particularly affect them, Zhang Jie's views on women's oppression are clearly different from those of western feminists. There are common points of course, but our consciousness has been formed by a different historical experience. This does not mean that she has nothing to offer us. On the contrary in *Leaden Wings* Zhang Jie provides us with a real insight into the lives and thinking of her skilfully-crafted characters and thus into contemporary Chinese society itself.